CHANGES

CHANGES

A Love Story

AMA ATA AIDOO

Afterword by Tuzyline Jita Allan

The Feminist Press
at The City University of New York
New York

Published 1993 by The Feminist Press at The City University of New
York, The Graduate Center, 365 Fifth Avenue, New York, NY 10016,
by arrangement with The Women's Press, London, England
feministpress.org

10 09 08 07 06   10 9 8 7 6

Library of Congress Cataloging-in-Publication Data

Aidoo, Ama Ata.
    Changes : a love story / Ama Ata Aidoo : afterword by Tuzyline
Jita Allan.
        p.   cm.
    ISBN-10: 1-55861-064-2 (hardcover) : —ISBN-10: 1-55861-065-0
(paperback), ISBN-13: 978-1-55861-065-1 (paperback)
    1. Women—Ghana—Accra—Fiction. 2. Man–woman
relationships—Ghana—Accra—Fiction. 3. Accra (Ghana)—
Fiction. I. Title
PR9379.9.A35C48   1993
823—dc20   93-29102
                                          ·   CIP

This publication is made possible, in part, by public funds from
the National Endowment for the Arts and the New York State
Council on the Arts. The Feminist Press would also like to thank
Sallie Bingham, Alida Brill, Joanne Markell, and Genevieve Vaughan
for their generosity.

Cover design by Paula Martinac

Printed in the United States on acid-free paper by McNaughton &
Gunn, Inc., Saline, Michigan.

For Kinna, my daughter, and some of my favorite
relatives:

> Jonathan Kariara
> Papa Kwamena Aidoo
> Fiifi Ayedan Aidoo

To the reader, a confession, and the critic, an apology

Several years ago when I was a little older than I am now, I said in a published interview that I could never write about lovers in Accra. Because surely in our environment there are more important things to write about? Working on this story then was an exercise in words-eating! Because it is a slice from the life and loves of a somewhat privileged young woman and other fictional characters — in Accra. It is not meant to be a contribution to any debate, however current.

AAA

Part I

1

Esi was feeling angry with herself. She had no business driving all the way to the offices of Linga Whatever. The car of course stalled more than once on the way, and, of course, all the other drivers were unsympathetic. They blew their horns, and some taxi drivers shouted the usual obscenities about 'women drivers'.

In spite of how strongly she felt about it all, why couldn't she ever prevent her colleagues from assuming that any time the office secretary was away, *she* could do the job? And better still, why couldn't she prevent herself from falling into that trap?

'Can I help you?' She was a bit startled. After she had parked her car and entered an open door, she had been quite surprised to find herself in an empty office. She had consulted her watch, and learned that in fact it was long past five o'clock in the evening. So she was wondering how the office had come to be open, as well as silently scolding herself, when the voice spoke.

She looked up into a very handsome face. Its owner knew it was handsome, too, plus one or two other flattering facts about himself. But Esi was not in any mood to notice looks or be charmed by self-consciously charming men.

'I'm from the Department of Urban Statistics,' she began, trying not to let her irritation show. 'Two of my colleagues and I are attending a conference in Lusaka on Thursday . . .'

'Eh,' she continued, 'I understand that normally this agency handles all travel arrangements for our office. But our secretary reported sick this morning, and since we don't know when she will be well enough to return to work, we thought maybe I could come and sort things out.'

But there is nothing tragic about that, is there? he wanted to ask. However, aloud, he asked her to follow him to his office. Inside, Esi felt the coolness of the air-conditioning immediately, and couldn't help reacting to it.

'Please sit down,' said the man, indicating a chair from a group of rather plush and low office furniture in the centre of the room. She was aware of feeling grateful that he had not asked her to sit by his rather imposing desk. The chair by the desk looked high and not so comfortable. She sat down, sighing audibly with relief. He eased himself into the armchair opposite her. Then he jumped up again.

'Forgive me,' he virtually drawled. 'I'm Ali Kondey, and the managing director of Linga . . . I mean this agency . . . Please, can I have the pleasure of knowing to whom I'm speaking?' It was Esi's turn to feel apologetic.

'Oh, I'm sorry, I didn't introduce myself. 'My name is Esi Sekyi.' They shook hands.

Still standing, Ali asked Esi if he could get her anything to drink. She was almost tempted to ask for water, at least, but she didn't. She was thinking that since she was too late for the trip to be useful in any way, why not just get out of that office as quickly as she could and get home before dark? She said as much to Ali, who was somewhat disappointed, but didn't think he should press the invitation.

'May I sit down?' he asked Esi, who thought the request so odd she burst out laughing.

'Why is that funny?' he asked, genuinely perplexed.

'It is your office, and quite obviously your chair. Why ask me if you might sit in it?'

'Well you see,' he began to explain, and then changed his mind. One area of communication that always made him feel sad were these walls which the different colonial experiences seemed to have erected between the different groups of Africans . . . especially when he hit them in relation to women.

Already seated, he said rather lamely, 'Never mind. But about what you were saying . . . do you know whether your secretary had already supplied my people with any specific information, like the day you would want to travel and when you are likely to come back?'

'Oh yes, I believe she must have sent in everything. I just thought I should come and check on the tickets and flight bookings.' Esi was talking, but she had a distinct impression that Ali was not really listening.

'*Alors, Madame,* don't worry about anything. They will do everything, my people, everything will be ready, prompt, for your journey, I promise. What I don't know is which of them is handling the arrangements for you and your colleagues. But it will all be okay.' His voice was virtually lulling her to sleep. When she got up to leave, saying that in that case, she better be going, she felt as if she were waking from a trance. It was unbelievable. Meanwhile, Ali was not finished with her yet. He too had already jumped up.

'In that case, let me finish locking up this office and drop you where you are going, please? . . . It would be a pleasure.'

'You are very kind, Mr Eh, Kondey, but actually I came in my car.' Esi became aware that something quite new and interesting was trying to make itself felt in that room that early evening, late in the month of June. She was not quite sure she wanted to welcome it or even identify it. Therefore, since she knew silences sometimes have a way of screaming strange messages, she spoke, to fill the air with words.

> They know that art well
> who trade in food –
> pad up
> where resources are scarce, or
> just for cool profit:
> grains for sausages
> some worms for burgers
> more leaves for *kenkey*!

'You see,' Esi went on, 'my car is here. Except that it isn't too good. In fact, it stopped a couple of times on the road. But . . .'

'Ah . . .' said Ali who had been struggling to deal with a solid feeling of disappointment, 'in that case, leave it here, and come with me in my car. I shall get it to your house for you early in the morning.'

What an alarming proposal, Esi was thinking. 'No, thank you

3

again, Mr Kondey, but that would just be too complicated,' she said aloud.

By now they were out of his office and in the main office of the agency and business arena. They came straight out into the open, and he locked the office. Ali recognised what for Esi passed for a car, and a tiny smile came playing around his lips. He killed a comment. And in any case Esi was talking, with an extended hand.

'Bye, Mr Kondey . . . thank you very much . . . and I hope your people will get in touch.' Then she was opening the door of her car, sitting before the wheel, putting it into motion, and with the old machine coughing like some asthmatic, she was gone.

Ali, who was completely fascinated with the sheer swiftness of her performance, caught himself saying, 'But of course . . . but of course.' Then there was really nothing else for him to do but get himself home.

This was a Friday evening. As a strictly brought-up Muslim who had actually gone to the mosque earlier in the afternoon, there was only one way to interpret his encounter with this fascinating woman: a gift from Allah. So he should not let himself feel too bad about the way the encounter had ended. If it was His will, things would right themselves in the end.

At that moment, the southern sky was ripped by massive lightning, followed by a heavy boom of thunder. As he got into his solid and luxurious vehicle, Ali had only one fear; that the threatening storm might sweep that woman and her car away. They both looked so frail.

2

Later, when she was much much grown, Ogyaanowa
was to ask herself what she would have preferred if she had been
consulted:

staying in their room and watching her parents fight;
or sitting outside at the dining table, pretending
to eat porridge and hearing them quarrel.

Actually, that morning, no one had consulted her. She had had to
eat the porridge as part of having to get ready to go to school. She
wished she didn't have to go to school. She wished she had already
gone to school. She wished, maybe, she hadn't had even to wake
up. She didn't know that morning that she was thinking of these
things. All she knew was that she was very unhappy.

Just ask anybody. There are many thoughts that come
into our minds which we are not aware of, at the time
we are doing the thinking. Feelings can be even worse.

Ogyaanowa didn't feel like eating any porridge that morning.
Therefore an accident happened, and the bowl of porridge fell off
the table. The bowl, which was plastic, rolled away, building a
solid line of porridge on the floor. Ogyaanowa started to cry.

The commotion that was coming out of her parents' room was
terrible. They had turned the radio on, thinking the noise from it
drowned their voices. It didn't though. True, if you were trying to
listen from where Ogyaanowa was sitting, you wouldn't have been
able to make out the words; although you would also have known
that something was going on that was not quite normal. But for the
child this had become quite regular. At least, that is what she might
have said if anyone had asked her about it, and if she had had a more
grown-up language.

When Esi opened the door to the bedroom, she was quite surprised to see Oko still in bed.

> Strange, she thought, for a man who takes his work as seriously as he does.

She unwrapped the cloth from her body, moved to the dressing table, took what she would need and brought the things to her side of the bed: some cream for her skin, a deodorant stick, a very mild toilet spray. She sat down, and picking these one by one, she started getting her body ready for the day.

As for the day, it was very young; but already the breeze that was blowing was maturely hot, as expected. In the course of it, for the next ten hours or so, there might be slight variations in temperature, a centigrade down, a few fahrenheits up. No one would take notice.

As she picked this up and poured a bit of that into her palm and rubbed it on parts of her body, Oko looked at her. Lying down and watching her go through the motions of dressing was a pleasure he was fully enjoying this particular morning. It occurred to him then, as it had occurred to him on countless other mornings before, that Esi had not lost a bit of her schoolgirl looks or schoolgirl ways.

For a teacher in a co-educational school, and soon to be a headmaster of one, this is a very dangerous thought indeed. He scolded himself.

Esi was a tall woman. That fact made a short man of Oko, since people mostly expect any man to be taller than his wife, and he was the same height as her. She was quite thin too, which gave her an elegance that was recognised by all except members of her own family. When she was younger and growing up in the big compound with her cousins and other members of the extended family, she had had to be extremely careful about starting a quarrel with anyone. Because no one lost the chance to call her beanpole, bamboo, pestle or any such name which in their language described tall, thin and uncurved.

> I love this body. But it is her sassy navel that kills me, thought Oko, watching the little protrusion, and feeling some heating up at the base of his own belly.

If Esi's mother could have read his thoughts, she would have told him that that dainty affair had nearly killed her daughter. For, instead of healing after a couple of weeks, like any baby's, Esi's had taken its time, going almost septic at one point. Meanwhile, as every old lady in the village reminded her throughout her childhood, Esi had been such a grouchy, wailing infant, her tummy had normally looked like a pumped balloon. So that even when the navel healed, it still stuck out.

Soon, the bedroom filled out with a mixture of scents.

'Aren't you getting up at all this morning?' Esi finally asked. Following her question, relief flooded through her like the effect of a good drink. For these days communication between them had ground to a halt, each of them virtually afraid of saying anything that might prove to be potentially explosive. And these days nearly everything was.

She needn't have worried. Oko had, on his own, decided that the months of frustrations and misunderstandings were behind him. Even hopefully behind them both. In any case, he had decided to give the relationship another chance.

If you are being honest with yourself, you would admit that you have always given this relationship a chance, he told himself.

Thinking of how much he had invested in the marriage with Esi, and how much he had fought to keep it going made him feel a little angry and a little embarrassed. With all that going on in his head, his penis, which had by then become really big and hard, almost collapsed. But since his eyes were still on Esi's navel, the thing jerked itself up again.

He had always loved Esi. And what was wrong with that?

'It's not safe to show a woman you love her . . . not too much anyway,' some male voice was telling him. But whose voice was that? His father's? His Uncle Amoa's? He wasn't sure that the voice belonged to any of those two. Of course those men and their kind hid their hearts very well. They were brought up to know how. On the other hand, they were also brought up too well to go around saying anything crude. No, it must have been one of his friends from boarding school days. They were always saying things of that sort. 'Showing a woman you love her is like asking her to walk over you. How much of your love for how heavy her kicks.' And were they wrong? Look at Esi. Two solid years of courtship, six years of marriage. And what had he got out of it? Little. Nothing. No affection. Not even plain warmth. Nothing except one little daughter! Esi had never stated it categorically that she didn't want any more children. But she was on those dreadful birth control things: pills, loops or whatever. She had gone on them soon after the child was born, and no amount of reasoning and pleading had persuaded her to go off them. He wanted other children, at least one more . . . a boy if possible. But even one more girl would have been welcome.

The fact that his mother and his sisters were always complaining to him about the unsafety of having an only child only made him feel worse. One of them had even suggested that he did himself and them the favour of trying to be interested in other women. That way, he could perhaps make some other children 'outside'. The idea hadn't appealed to him at all. In fact, for a long time, the thought of sleeping with anyone other than Esi had left him quite cold, no matter how brightly the sun was shining, or how hot the day was. Yet, what was he to do? Esi definitely put her career well above any duties she owed as a wife. She was a great cook, who complained endlessly any time she had to enter the kitchen. Their home was generally run by an elderly house help, whom they both called 'Madam' behind her back.

The bungalow came with her job as a data analyst with the government's statistical bureau; its urban department, that is.

Good God, what on earth did that mean?

He knew she was very much respected by her colleagues and other people who knew the work she did. So she should not really be trying so hard to impress: leaving the house virtually at dawn; returning home at dusk; often bringing work home? Then there were all those conferences. Geneva, Addis, Dakar one half of the year; Rome, Lusaka, Lagos the other half.

Is Esi too an African woman? She not only is, but there are plenty of them around these days . . . these days . . . these days.

Esi rose, picked up her tubes and bottles to return them to the dressing table. Oko's voice stopped her.

'My friends are laughing at me,' he said.

Silence.

'They think I'm not behaving like a man.'

Esi was trying to pretend she had not heard the declaration.

'Aren't you saying anything?' Oko's voice was full of pleading.

'What would you like me to say?' she spoke at last, trying very hard to keep the irritation out of her voice.

'You don't care what my friends think of me?' he pressed.

When she spoke again, the irritation was out, strong and breathing. 'Oko, you know that we have been over this so many times. We all make friends. They either respect us for what we are, or they don't. And whether we keep them or not depends on each one of us. I cannot take care of what your friends say to you, think of you or do to you.'

'I need my friends,' he said.

'I also need mine,' she said.

'Opokuya is a good woman,' he said.

Esi yawned, groped for her wrist-watch from the table, and looked at it. Oko snatched the watch from her, and threw it on the bedside table on his side of the bed.

'What did you do that for?' Esi demanded.

For an answer, Oko flung the bedcloth away from him, sat up, pulled her down, and moved on her. Esi started to protest. But he went on doing what he had determined to do all morning. He squeezed her breast repeatedly, thrust his tongue into her mouth, forced her unwilling legs apart, entered her, plunging in and out of her, thrashing to the left, to the right, pounding and just pounding away. Then it was all over. Breathing like a marathon runner at the end of a particularly gruelling race, he got off her, and fell heavily back on his side of the bed. He tried to draw the bedcloth to cover both of them again.

For some time, neither of them spoke. There was nothing else he wanted to say, and there was nothing she could say, at least, not for a while.

What does one do with this much rage? This much frustration? This much deliberate provocation so early in the morning, and early in the week?

She could go back to the bathroom and clean herself with a wet towel, just standing by the handbasin. She could go and run a full bath again and briefly soak her whole self up. Either way, she could be out of the house in another half-an-hour, drop Ogyaanowa at her school and be only a little late for work. Or she could forget about going to work altogether, wait until Oko had got himself up and taken the child to school, and then have a good cry. She preferred the latter option, but dared not take it. Not show up at work at all the whole day? And a Monday too? Impossible. It was bad enough that she was going to be late. A woman in her kind of job must be careful . . .

In the meantime, Oko was collecting his thoughts together. He was already feeling like telling Esi that he was sorry. But he was also convinced he mustn't. He got out of bed, taking the entire sleeping cloth with him. Esi's anger rose to an exploding pitch. Not just because Oko taking the cloth left her completely naked, or because she was feeling uncomfortably wet between her thighs. What really finished her was her eyes catching sight of the cloth trailing behind Oko who looked like some arrogant king, as he opened the door to get to the bathroom before her. She sucked her teeth, or made the noise which is normally described, inadequately, in English as a sucking of the teeth. It was thin, but loud, and very long. In a contest with any of the fishwives about ten kilometres down the road from the Hotel Twentieth Century, she would have won.

One full hour later, she was easing her car into the parking lot of the Department of Urban Statistics. The car came to a standstill. She turned off the engine, removed the keys from the ignition, dumped them irritably into her handbag, got out of the vehicle with an unconscious and characteristic haste, and literally ran to her office on the third floor of the building. This morning, she did not even bother to find out whether the lift was working. Since if it was, it would have been maybe only the sixth or seventh time the whole year, and most probably the last time before the end of the century.

Once in her office, she sat down, first to get her breath back. Then she just sat, uncharacteristically doing nothing at all. She became aware that she was in no hurry to do any work inside her office, or go out and meet anybody. In fact, she was rather surprised at the degree of lethargy she was feeling. She could not remember when last had she felt so clearly unwilling to face the world . . . and then with a kind of shock, she realised that in spite of the second bath she had had before leaving home, she was still not feeling fresh or clean.

Clean? It all came to her then. That what she had gone through with Oko had been marital rape.

'Marital rape?!' She began to laugh rather uncontrollably, and managed to stop herself only when it occurred to her that anyone coming upon her that minute would think she had lost her mind, which would not have been too far from the truth. In fact, her professional self was coldly telling her that she was hysterical. And isn't hysteria a form of mental derangement? At that she got up and went to lock the door.

She could hardly remember what commitments were on her schedule for the day. Yes, there was some data analysing she and her colleague had to do for the Minister. But that, mercifully, was for three o'clock that afternoon.

Marital rape. She sat down again, this time almost making herself comfortable. As if the state paid her to come and sit in her office to try and sort out her personal life! One part of her was full of disapproval, while the other – a kind of brand new self – could not have cared less.

Marital rape. Suddenly, she could see herself or some other woman sociologist presenting a paper on:

'The Prevalence of Marital Rape in the
Urban African Environment'

to a packed audience of academics. Overwhelmingly male, of course. A few women. As the presentation progresses, there are boos from the men, and uncomfortable titters from the women. At the end of it, there is predictable hostile outrage.

'Yes, we told you, didn't we? What is burying us now are all these imported feminists ideas . . .'

'And, dear lady colleague, how would you describe "marital rape" in Akan?'

'Igbo? . . . Yoruba?'

'Wolof? . . . or Temne?'

'Kikuyu? . . . or Ki-Swahili?'

'Chi-Shona?'

'Zulu? . . . or Xhosa?'

Or . . .

She was caught in her own trap. Hadn't she some long time ago said in an argument that

> 'you cannot go around claiming that an idea or an
> item was imported into a given society unless
> you could also conclude that to the best of your
> knowledge, there is not, and never was any word or
> phrase in that society's indigenous language which
> describes that idea or item'?

By which and other proof, the claims that 'plantain', 'cassava' and other African staples came from Asia or the Americas could only be sustained by racist historians and lazy African academics? And both suffering from the same disease: allergy to serious and honest research. . . . African staples coming from the Americas? Ha, ha, ha! . . . And incidentally, what did the slaves take there with them by way of something to grow and eat? . . . What a magnificent way to turn history on its head! . . . She told herself that when it came to poor history getting turned on its head, there was too much of that sort of thing going on around Africa and Africans anyway . . .

But marital rape? No. The society could not possible have an indigenous word or phrase for it. Sex is something a husband claims from his wife as his right. Any time. And at his convenience. Besides, any 'sane' person, especially sane women, would consider any other woman lucky or talented or both, who can make her husband lose his head like that.

> What does she use? Some well-known stuff?
> It must be a new product from Europe or America . . .
> You know how often she travels.
> 'Ei, Esi Sekyi . . . and she always looks so busily
> professional . . . and so booklong!'

And here she was, not feeling academic or intellectual at all, but angry, and sore . . . And even after a good bath before and after, still dirty . . . Dirty! . . . Ah-h-h-h, the word was out.

She put her head on her desk. She must have dozed off for a

minute or two. She woke up with a start, and somewhat disorientated. When her mind cleared, she realised that she had made a decision.

3

Compared to Esi, Opokuya was definitely fat. Not that she cared. She moved like lightning, and laughed through the days of the year. Any time the question of her obesity cropped up, she made it quite clear that the fact that she was fat had nothing to do with not knowing what to do about it. She had been a state registered nurse and a qualified midwife for nearly fifteen years. In those years, she had concluded that those who are interested in women, especially African women, losing so much weight must be the same ones who are interested in women, especially African women, cutting down their birth rate.

'You Opokuya. As for you Opokuya,' her listeners would protest.

'I could be wrong,' she would make an attempt to concede, and then move straight on, 'otherwise how is it that no matter how remote and hidden a rural clinic is, two items you are bound to find in great amounts are pamphlets and samples for losing weight and contraception? Eh?' she would ask her bemused listeners, her hands akimbo. ' . . . And as for hospitals like this one, you know we would never run out of the routine drugs if they were also contraceptive and we gave them to all patients, including men and children, and asked them to take them three times a day before meals.' She would glare around, her eyes blazing in a most unnatural way. When she got into such deep areas, people normally kept quiet and listened to her.

'Meanwhile, our governments are behaving like all professional beggars. They have learned the rules of effective begging, one of them being that you never object to anything the giver likes. And they know the givers like one thing very much now: that there should not be too many of us. Under such circumstances, how does the beggar tell the giver to go and stuff his dangerous and experimental contraceptive pills, capsules and injections? Yes, injections. And they call their murderous programmes such beautiful names: "family planning" and "mother health"... all to cover up...'

Her listeners were nearly always hospital personnel. Some thought they recognised the truth of what she was saying. Others simply felt embarrassed, wondering what a decently married woman was doing with such mad ideas in her head. Some of them would turn away when she was carrying on. Some would keep quiet. But there were always others who stayed and continued to argue with her in an effort to get her to see modern and civilised reason.

Opokuya had thought quite hard about the politics of population and fat. She had concluded that the way population, especially, was being handled in relation to Africans left her frightened. It seemed to her that any time someone else showed such a keen interest in your not making children, then for sure, he is not just interested in your good health, your prosperity, and the good health and prosperity of your children. For herself, Opokuya had decided she wanted four children. She had had them, and then brought the matter out in the open to discuss with her husband, Kubi. After they had agreed that, indeed, four were enough, she had gone to one of the gynaecologists she respected, sorted things out with him, booked herself on to his surgery schedule, and for a bed in the gynae ward. She had then gone in to have the ends of her fallopian tubes tied or singed, whatever. Finish!

Opokuya had not so far been able to sort out the weight issue that neatly, even in relation to herself. She would admit once in a while that she was a little bothered about the possibility of a heart complication. She routinely took her blood pressure, which remained remarkably normal. Besides, since she didn't know the extent to which her body was capable of expanding, she had a long time ago taught herself to do without the more obvious criminal items like sugar and fatty foods. So it was that knowledge and this discipline which gave her the confidence to argue so hotly. Sometimes she truly felt like a fraud.

No two humans could have been as different, physically and temperamentally, as Opokuya and Esi. But they also got on very very well. In fact, they had been friends for so long, and they had become so close, their mothers related to one another like friends and sisters too, in spite of the fact that they lived in different parts of the country.

Opokuya and Kubi had met when she was a student nurse, and they had got married the year she had graduated from nursing school. Her midwifery qualification was to come later.

Their oldest child, a girl, was just a little younger than her mother's first professional certificate. She and the next child after her, a boy, were in secondary boarding schools. The two youngest, also boys, were still in primary school, and lived with their parents.

Opokuya and Kubi lived on Sweet Breezes Hill. It had been the most prestigious of the colonial residential areas. They occupied the same old colonial surveyor's bungalow built in the 1930s, and Opokuya was always quite aware of the different spirits who also inhabited the house. There was that of the first surveyor who had probably selected the hill as the site most suitable for occupation by them, the English civil servants who were sent to these deadly mosquito-infested regions to administer the territories on behalf of their royal majesties, and generally civilise the natives. These natives, both the groups on this part of the Guinea coast, and in the interior of the country, were reputed to be some of the rudest and most untameable throughout the whole of the British Empire. Why this was so, no one knew, but it was definitely so. In time, quite a sizeable group of Englishmen had come bringing their women with them. They had lived close to one another so that they would be well-placed to fight those natives with guns, the mosquitoes with alcohol, and general boredom with women. Of course, they always could and they often did import both alcohol and women from 'home'. But then, there had also been more than adequate local supplies of both. So in the end they banned the local liquor to force the natives to buy expensive English gin and Scottish whisky, and then proceeded to take over the local women.

Other spirits inhabited the Dakwa's house which were perhaps more kindred. Though sometimes she wondered whether they

16

could be said to be more benevolent just because they were African.

'It's up to them,' she murmured to herself.

'You aren't talking to yourself, are you?' said Kubi, as he returned to their bedroom from eating his breakfast.

'Oh, you frightened me so,' Opokuya protested. 'But I probably was talking to myself,' she confessed.

'And what is the problem now?' Kubi was quite sensitive to Opokuya's moods.

'I'm not sure myself. In any case, I think the conversations I hold with myself which occasionally appear on my lips don't really have anything to do with what you call "my problems".'

'But what is it this morning?' Kubi pursued.

'Probably same as yesterday's.'

'Which is?'

'How to co-ordinate the car's movements.'

The problem was out. Knowing it was one of the few areas of friction in their otherwise good marriage, Opokuya hated bringing it up. But she had to: every morning. Yet both of them saw the issue of the car's movements as being 'very simple'. Kubi felt that like his colleagues in the office and the civil service generally, he should be able to drive his car to his place of work. Especially since the government paid for its fuel consumption and general maintenance, and anyway, in most regional offices there was always a place in the car-park, marked out for the surveyor's car. He was convinced that the car should be parked there all day. He would move it at half past twelve to go home for lunch. Then he would drive it back at a quarter to two, park it, let it stand for the rest of the afternoon, until he was ready to drive home at the end of a working day. Whenever there was a day's field trip, he insisted that the car should stand on its spot the whole day, until he returned from the bush or wherever and drove it home in the evening. Opokuya should go to work and return home with the hospital vans.

Opokuya thought this was absolutely ridiculous and even mad. A car is to be used. How was she to work full-time, and medical work at that, and look after a family as big as theirs without transportation of her own? Was he aware of the amount of running around one had to do to feed and clothe four growing children?

'It's a question of ethics!'

'W-h-a-a-a-t?'

'Yes, it's a question of ethics.'

'What ethics? It's common sense.'

'What do you mean common sense? Are you abusing me? I collect my full car maintenance allowance. Do you want me to let you drive it every day to the market?'

'But –'

'Does the fact that everybody else does it mean that we should do it too?'

'Please, Kubi, listen. First of all, I am not abusing you. And you know I'm not trying to say that you should let me drive the car all over the place with government maintenance –'

'Then what are you saying?'

'If you would let me finish. Please, just take your car off maintenance –'

'What? What an idea! I'm a senior civil servant. Car maintenance is an approved fringe benefit.'

'What I'm trying to say is that since I also need the car in order to look after the family properly, please take the car off maintenance. With your salary and mine, we should be able to take care of the car ourselves. That way, there would be no reason for any of us to feel guilty when I drive it.'

'You always carry on as if you are the only salary-earner around.'

'Oh,' she would say with all the affection she felt for her husband packed into her voice, 'now you are being unfair. You know I am not talking about the money. I'm just talking about the up-and-down I have to do each day to keep us going.'

Whenever Opokuya complained about her husband's 'unreasonable attitude' about the car to any of her female colleagues, they would nod sympathetically in front of her, and laugh at her behind her back. As far as they were concerned, it was Opokuya who was unreasonable or mad. Clearly, she didn't know anything. She should listen to the stories of women who paid for cars which their husbands then took over completely. In some cases, whisking their girlfriends around town in them.

For the whole world to see.
'Definitely for the whole world to see, and
sometimes even refusing the wife a ride,
if he should pass her on the street.'
'Opokuya is just spoilt.'
'She is really spoilt.'
Opokuya didn't know that she was supposed to be spoilt. She did
not feel spoilt. Each morning's argument ended with one of them
giving in. The winner drove the car. When it was Kubi, which was
most days, he would deposit Opokuya at the hospital and then take
the car, whistling all the way to the regional administrative
offices. If Opokuya won, she would deposit Kubi in front of his
office and drive away from there, humming all the way. Then once
she had found a good parking place, she would park, remain seated
in the car, mentally look through her day, and quickly make a list.
She always knew that even in a week with the car there was no
chance of her being able to do half of what she had put down for the
day. But she would put everything down anyway.

One area of relief for both of them was the result of a decision
they had made quite early in their life together. They would not
make a habit of dropping their kids at school and bringing them
home in the evening. They would do that only when the children
were in nurseries and kindergartens. But not after. So the children
daily made their way on the city buses, just like most of the other
kids from the neighbourhood. It was different when the bus broke
down, which was uncomfortably often. On such occasions, they
did take the children to school, and brought them back home at the
end of the school day.

'So what is it that you absolutely must do today?' Kubi asked
with his 'I-am-trying-to-be-sensible-and-you-must-also-try'
voice. Opokuya refused to take the bait.

'Kubi, you know quite well that there are at least a dozen things
I must "absolutely" do today,' she replied with her, 'this-morning-
I-don't-have-the-time-to-treat-a-fully-grown-man-like-some-
mother's- spoilt-boy-voice'.

'Opokuya just name me one,' he commanded.

Opokuya decided to comply, patiently, 'Do you remember that

you and I had agreed that while I am away visiting my mother, the children would go to your sister's?'

'Yes,' Kubi agreed, rather cautiously.

'Well, we cannot just go and dump the kids on her on my way to the bus depot the morning I'm leaving. It won't be right even though Connie is the most reasonable of all your sisters. We have to warn her.'

'M . . . hm,' Kubi was getting more and more cautious. Apart from the fact that he had not really agreed with himself that it was necessary for her to go and visit her mother, years of having a clever woman in his home and an unbroken chain of rather stupid heads of department in his place of work had taught him not to take anything for granted in a discussion.

'You see,' Opokuya continued, 'I thought I would have the car for today, so that I could go by her place from the hospital and discuss it with her.'

Kubi relaxed. He could win this one. In fact, he would. Opokuya was starting her accumulated leave the next week. She was planning on going to spend the bigger portion of it visiting her family. But between that morning and the first day of her leave, there was at least a week within which there was nothing she could not do if she put her mind to it. With, or without the car: including going to ask the sister to take the kids on . . .

'Listen, it looks like I'm already going to be late for our budget meeting this morning.'

Opokuya knew she had lost, and there was no point in asking him how it was that the Regional Survey Department had a budget meeting every morning of every week. Without saying another word, she picked up her handbag and her basket, and went to sit in the car. After elaborately checking on the tyres and the water level, Kubi went to sit in the driving seat. During the four good kilometres' journey from Sweet Breezes Hill to the city's main and general hospital, they did not speak to one another. Another of the patterns of the mornings when she lost the car. Since she refused to start a conversation, and he was sure she would not even join in if he did, they both kept quiet.

When he parked by the hospital gate, he asked a little guiltily, 'We'll meet in the house this evening?'

20

'No,' she snapped back, 'I shall not come home with the hospital van. I'll find my way to your sister's anyway.'

'Shall I come and get you from there then?'

'You don't have to bother,' she said again, barely managing to suppress her fury. 'You know it's too far out. And you should be feeling tired if it's going to be one of your exhausting meetings.'

'So how are you going to get back home?' said Kubi, genuine concern joining guilt, and neither escaping Opokuya's notice.

'I could come into town with the bus, and wait at the Hotel Twentieth Century for you . . .'

'Okay,' said Kubi. He hated having to stop in town after work. But he was aware that he had to make some concessions.

'From about half past five,' Opokuya reminded him. They both knew what she was talking about.

Opokuya was already out of the car. In fact, the last bit of the exchange was done with her holding the door of the car, ready to bang it shut. She now shut it and turned to walk towards the hospital. Kubi reversed left, turned right to face the road and then turned right again. He was on his way to work. Whistling, of course.

4

How people described the stature of Ali Kondey depended entirely on where they stood in relation to the Gulf of Guinea. Right on the coast and in the forest regions he was considered tall. In the sparse grasslands of the middle belt, they thought of his height as 'medium'. In the upper regions and Sub-Sahel, he was seen as not being so tall. In fact, in such areas some could say he was short. But there was no such doubt anywhere about his skin. It was smooth and black, and not a layer of fat between that skin and his flesh. His teeth, which he occasionally, deliberately and fashionably discoloured by chewing kola, were beautifully even and white. He wore kohl around his eyes, moved like a panther, and was very good looking. He knew all this himself, including the fact that he was the most effective advertisement for Linga HideAways, the travel and tourist agency he had established soon after his country became independent.

Ali's country? Which one was that?

Ali was a son of the world. He had dropped out of his mother's womb absolutely determined to come and live this life. As his other mothers on both sides of his family would later let him know whenever they had the chance, the burden of bringing him into this world had been too much for his mother. Poor Fatimatu.

'Was she not fifteen when Ali was born?'

'That was all she was.'

'Then how could she have lived?'

'She could not live. She did not live.

I saw it all. She looked at the baby Ali very well.

You would have thought she just wanted to be sure

that everything was fine with him.'

'Then what happened?'
'Ah my sister, may Allah preserve us. She sat
quietly and bled to death.'

In the commotion that had followed that catastrophe, Ali had been nearly forgotten. Indeed, the only one who seemed to have remembered his existence had been himself. He yelled and kept yelling until someone had picked him up, cleaned him and found him some breasts with milk in them. He never forgot the experience ever! And for months he never really stopped crying, completely convinced that if he stopped, he would be forgotten again.

Like most men everywhere and from time immemorial – who have been able to pay for the luxury – Ali's father preferred his women young and tender. They had to be virgins, of course. And he had acquired one such woman for a wife in each of his eight favourite stops on his trade routes. At the time, and at fourteen, Ali's mother had been his youngest and his current favourite. He had tried to have her travelling with him, something he had not done with any other woman before her, and she turned out to be the last. For, much to his disappointment, she soon became pregnant and there had been nothing he could do about it. What he had done, however, was take her to his sister, who was living in Bamako and married to a tailor. She was known as Mma Danjuma, after Danjuma, her oldest child, who was about two years old when Ali was born.

Ali's father left him with Mma Danjuma, and for the first eight years or so of his life, Mma Danjuma looked after the orphan so well, people did not think they should even try to find out whether he really was her son, or whether what they had heard was true. Ali was Mma's child. That was why, when he had come to choose a home, he had decided on Bamako. Not just because that's where he had been told he had been born, but that was where Mma lived. Bamako was home. Then, having settled that question for the convenience of his heart, he had proceeded to claim the entire Guinea Coast, its hinterland and the Sub-Sahel for his own. In any case, since he had learned that his grandfather's house had stood on the exact spot where Burkina Faso, Ghana and Togo met, he had assumed the nationalities of Ghana, Benin, Côte d'Ivoire, Burkina

Faso, Niger, Mali, Nigeria and Togo. Naturally, he carried a passport to prove the genuineness of each.

Ali's father had lived, travelled and traded through them all: Ghana when it was the Gold Coast, Burkina when it was Upper Volta, and even earlier, from the days of 'French West Africa'. He had gone on horseback; camels; deathtraps that called themselves taxis; the back of ancient lorries and all other things that moved and could carry a fully-grown man – including his own two feet.

'My father bought everything from everybody, and could sell anything to anybody,' boasted Ali, laughing and touching his heart, while his eyes danced clear in their pools of kohl. And if it ever occurred to Ali that the women he seduced so easily fell more in love with the picture he painted of his father for them, and not so much for himself, it didn't bother him too much. Ali loved his father completely, and was very proud of the part of himself that met his father's approval, as well as that part of himself which he knew, secretly, resembled his father. Above all he was aware that establishing Linga was just continuing the family trade, with a little more organisation, modernisation and a whole lot of elegance. Of course, he had offices in all his countries, with the headquarters in Accra.

The only way in which Ali was not like his father, and did not seem to care, was in the area of women. Ali liked his women mature, and he had no special use for virginity, especially in very young girls.

Musa Musa had been the name Ali's father had been known by throughout the whole of West Africa before Ali was born. Of course, after Ali was born, and became old enough to travel with him sometimes, Musa Musa quickly came to be known as 'Ali Baba', and that stuck. Musa Musa's father, Musa Kondey, that is Ali's grandfather, who was long dead by the time Ali was born, had been quite rich. He had owned an impressive number of sons, cattle, horses, sheep, goats, wives and daughters. All definitely in that order of value. Since he had not been the head of his clan, he could not have owned the largest numbers of any of those commodities. But he had been a minor prince, which also meant that he would have been much wealthier than those of his contemporaries who had not been princes. Musa Musa had been one of several children from one of his father's middle wives.

One day, when he was about twelve years old, he had taken his share of the sheep and goats out to graze, as was expected of him. Early in the afternoon he had eaten his packed lunch and drunk his day's ration of water. Soon after, he had felt sleepy, and had walked into a thicket that had become something of a favourite spot, and dozed. Just for a short while. Sleeping on the job was something his father punished most severely, if caught. On that particular afternoon, Musa Musa had been startled awake by the barking of his dog. He had looked around and realised that what appeared to be a small lion was running away with a goat. He was too frightened even to come out of his thicket until a while later, when the baby lion was long gone. When he did emerge and counted his animals, sure enough one kid was missing. He burst into tears. After the tears, he asked himself what he was to do. He knew that at the end of the day the animals would be counted. He knew the loss would be discovered. He also knew his father and his punishment for losing an animal. So what was he to do? The kid was gone. By evening, when he was ready to return the animals home, he had decided. He drove the animals close enough to the kraal so that it would not be difficult for the dog to take them home. Then he disappeared.

The next time Musa Musa ventured home, he was over forty and greying from his temples. In the meantime, he had become one of the biggest door-to-door traders of the entire sub-region. There was nothing he did not carry to sell: from safety pins, hair pins and zips to giant funerary masks and statues of gods and goddesses – some phoney and newly created, others old and authentic. These last were stolen by his enterprising contacts from royal mausoleums and sacred shrines. Later, much later, when all the countries had become independent and tourism to that part of Africa was very much in fashion, Musa Musa had set up his own group of carvers. These were his youngest brothers and nephews. The latter were the sons of his numerous sisters, and more than anything else, it was his intention to set them up in business that had taken him back to his village. His father was already dead, so there was no chance of anyone expecting him to come up with an explanation for anything . . . especially a goat lost over thirty years ago!

It had been established without doubt that it was indeed him, Musa Musa. His mother, now an old woman, had remembered the tragedy of losing him and cried, and then cried some more for the joy of having him back. The next day a great feast of welcoming had been organised so that everyone could celebrate and have a nice time. A lost person does not find his way home every day.

Depending on where he himself was heading, Musa Musa's carvers would make any piece of wood yield any desired image. Sanufu antelope dancing headdresses, Akuaba dolls, Igbo, Yoruba and Baluba masks. He had added to his carver's skills the art of curing wood in such a way that freshly sculptured pieces felt, looked and smelled more real and much more old than the really ancient pieces Ali used to buy.

'I'm grateful to my old man,' Ali would later say to Esi. 'Leaving me that group and their skills is worth more than a million dollars in the bank, you know.' He would laugh, touch his heart and continue: 'Besides, knowing my father, he would have hated the tiresome business of having to put a good story together to explain how he could suddenly have come into such money, since all his life he had avoided the banks.'

'Was he into currency deals?' the listener would ask.

'But what a very rude question. In any case, how do you think people like my father could have managed to keep commerce and other economic activities thriving in this area if they had played in the white man's bank with their money?'

'But after independence?'

'What are you talking about? . . . My father keeps telling everyone openly that he will take his money to the bank the day something changes properly. As far as he is concerned, these independences have proved to be nothing more than a trick! You should see him imitating African leaders when they are with the heads of Western governments or their representatives, as they tremble and grin with great effort to please! And Allah, he can do them all! Francophone, Anglophone, Lusophone, any kind. No, he is convinced that nothing has changed, so he sleeps on his money.'

'So he is still alive?'

'Of course. And still marrying the fourteen-year-old girls.' Ali always pretended great shock at any suggestion that his father might die. He thought any discussion of that subject was in very bad taste, and Musa Musa agreed with him. Indeed the only opinion Musa Musa could possibly have shared with African heads of state is that any discussion of our mortality is treason and punishable, by death of course, if the circumstances are right.

Allah be praised.

Ali's house was a big structure at the entrance to Nima, from New Town. It had been built in the middle of the 1940s by a local man who had made a lot of money in the Second World War. None of the children this man had sent to England to be 'properly educated' had bothered to come back. So out of sheer frustration he had driven their different mothers out, and for several years had lived alone. Then, once he knew he was about to die, he had put the house up for sale to spite his family. He knew they were just waiting for him to die to begin harassing one another over the property. The only condition to go with the sale was that whoever bought the house should wait for him to be laid in his grave before taking possession. Which is exactly what happened. Ali had then thoroughly renovated it and built a proper wall around it.

Early in his sojourn in the south, Ali had decided that he would always live in the *zongo* of the cities in which he found himself. He had not tried to analyse that decision into its parts except to say that, 'for one, *zongo* is the only area in these places where one can be sure of always getting some decent *tuo*'. If the house he had bought was not exactly in Nima, he could at least console himself with the thought that it was near enough. From his favourite corner on the balcony upstairs, he could hear and see that city-within-city buzzing with maximum activity during the day, and winking all over at night – also with maximum activity. Nima never slept.

Ali had first come south with his father when he was about four years old. Musa Musa always stayed in Nima, with different friends and relatives, deciding on which household, according to how he felt on each trip. When he began to take Ali with him on a regular basis, there was a routine he always followed – in Nima as well as in all the other cities and towns on his routes. As soon as he arrived, he would promptly put Ali in a Koranic school. By the time he was eight, Ali could recite more than double the verses normally expected from one his age. This worked out to about ten chapters of the Holy Book. From Bamako down through Ouga and Kumasi, from Abidjan across Sekondi, Accra and Lome, all his teachers proclaimed him an exceptionally bright pupil.

One day, when Ali was nearly nine years old and they were in Bamako, his mother Mma Danjuma did 'one of her things'. After the whole family had returned from the mosque and her brother and her husband were swearing by Allah that they would surely die any minute from hunger, Mma disappeared into the huge kitchen which she shared with the other tenants' wives. Then she called her two older boys, Danjuma and Ali – but not, as the boys expected, because she had heated the food and she was going to dish it out for them to take to where the men were. Instead, she just pulled a chair out and sat down. Then she gave the boys some francs and told them to go to Monsieur Abdoulayi's and get the family some kola. The boys were very surprised. It was a most unusual command. The one thing they never ever ran out of in their corner of the compound was kola. Indeed, every now and then Mma herself sold kola to the other residents, since her brother always brought her a small sackful whenever he came from the south. Musa Musa meant the kola for her and her husband's use. But it was always a lot. Too much.

'How many mouths does Musa think we have, eh?' Mma would ask no one in particular. She would then proceed to give several away to her women friends, until one of them, a much more realistic somebody than Mma could ever be, asked whether Mma didn't think that if she sold some of the nuts, she could find something else, like salt, to buy with the money? That was a hint Mma took.

So to go and buy kola from someone else, especially when Ali and his father had just arrived from the south the night before, sounded very strange indeed. But then, grown-ups are always strange and unpredictable. Both boys said, 'Oui, Mma,' and left the house.

The boys were right. Mma didn't need the kola. She just wanted them out of the house for a short while. That was why, in her haste, she had named the first commodity that had come into her head.

28

'Ah-ah, there are things you don't discuss with young people listening in. Especially if it's about their future. Since they never forget, if they overhear you making decisions about them which later turn out to have been unfortunate, they would never forgive you . . .'

Mma adjusted her veil and approached the men. To their cries of 'Where is the food?' and 'Where is the *tuo*?' she asked them to be patient and wait. She knelt. Another surprise that afternoon. Mma never knelt.

'It's about Ali.'

'Uh . . . huh,' grunted the men.

'Musa, no one is a better father than you. The boy doesn't miss his mother. Allah be praised.'

'Ei,' exclaimed both men, 'what mother are you talking about now? Are you not the boy's mother?'

'Please forgive my words,' said Mma, nervously. She realised immediately that she had almost gone too far in her attempt to oil them up for what she was about to say. 'But the boy is growing. Now he knows enough Arabic to improve on his verses himself with the reading of the Holy Book.'

'Woman, woman, be short,' her husband, Baba Danjuma, cut in. 'What is it you want to tell your brother?' Baba Danjuma was trying to hide his fury that whatever it was, she had not discussed it with him first.

'Musa,' said Mma, 'I want you to leave Ali with us properly. No more travelling for him. So we can put him into a French school. Please? These days, that is very important. Koranic schools are all right. But . . .'

Musa and Baba Danjuma were already laughing a great deal and calling on Allah to come bless this good woman, their wife and their sister. But that was what they had been discussing all morning! Strange . . . Allah is great. They had thought they would tell her what they had agreed about Ali after she had fed them. Since, may Allah protect us all, if she did not hurry with the food, she might have two corpses to deal with . . . Ah no, there was no problem. Of course, Ali would go to the French school.

Mma Danjuma was very surprised, and relieved. She had nothing more to say. There was just no need. She rose up.

'Ah ... yah,' she said, 'I shall bring the food now.' She went back to the kitchen.

A little while later, when she took the steaming bowls in herself, Baba Danjuma thought there was something odd about it.

'Where are the boys?' he asked.

'I sent them to Abdoulayi,' she replied. Why explain further?

'Oh ... oh, both men murmured. They too were quite anxious to eat, they didn't feel like probing. Since they had already done their ablutions, they immediately attacked their food.

As Mma turned to return to the kitchen there was a smile on her face. Ah men, how easy that was! Had they really discussed sending Ali to the French school? Or had they just agreed quickly so that she, a woman, wouldn't have the credit of being the one to have brought out a good idea? Or was it just because they were anxious to eat? Mma knew she would never know the answer to that one. But what did it matter as long as they did not stand in her way and ruin her plans to get the boy properly educated? They are men. They must have their little self-deceptions.

In time, Ali went to the junior French school, and later, the lycée. Much later he continued to Ghana and went to a teacher training college, where he met Fusena his wife. Later still he gave up teaching and got himself to England, where he acquired both a bachelor's and a master's degree in Sociology and Economics.

When Ali was in an English-speaking environment, people found his language 'quaint' with its French accent and philosophical turn to everyday phrases. When he was in a Francophone environment, people thought his language enchantingly 'simple, comme les Anglais!'

5

Sunset over the Gulf of Guinea is something very special – any evening.

'Sister, the sea has melted,' said the seven-year-old Kweku to his aunt, as he gazed at the ocean under one such glory.

Driving towards the Hotel Twentieth Century, Esi was completely overwhelmed by the vision of so much gold, golden red and red filtering through the branches of the coconut palms. Although she herself had been born not that far from the sea, even she wondered, as she later looked for parking outside the hotel, how people who had such scenes at their backyards felt on a daily basis. Then, ashamed of herself for automatically applying a research approach, she told the sociologist in her to shut up.

The beach was only a couple of kilometres to the right of the hotel, and the fishermen who were busy packing up their boats down there might have been amused if they had heard her thoughts. For at that time, what they were wondering was whether the government would fulfil its promise to help them get motorised boats and better nets, and when the Minister of Power would stop increasing the price of kerosene; and that night out at sea, would it be warm? For definitely, a chillier wind than they were used to was blowing through their lives.

Having located a good place, Esi parked expertly, jumped out of the car, locked it, and strode towards the reception desk of the hotel, her shoes beating out the determination in her mind.

'Yes, Madam? Good evening, can I help you?' All that from one of the two men manning the place, said very hurriedly, almost as if he was afraid to pause in case Esi interrupted him before he had finished his standard greeting. She did not interrupt him. But once she was sure he had finished his recitation she asked him if a foreign friend who should be in for a conference had arrived.

'Oh, yes,' the receptionist cut in, quite affably though. 'You were here about the same time yesterday to ask for her?'

'Yes, yes,' Esi agreed, a little surprised that he could recall so instantly and so accurately.

'Just a minute,' said the man and with that he turned aside, picked up a clipboard that held some sheets and quickly read what was on the sheets. Then he looked up.

'There are three new arrivals for that workshop. What is the name of your friend?'

'Wambui Wanjiku,' her voice registering an anticipated disappointment, 'she is coming from Kenya.' The man looked at his sheet again, although he already knew the name was not on it. Then he looked up. 'No, she has not arrived yet.'

'No?'

'No.'

'Thanks.'

Esi turned around. She paused for a while and moved a step or two, towards the entrance. But she changed her mind about going back out. It was clear that she was uncertain as to what to do next. She could go and sit down to have a beer. But she knew this was not really done. A woman alone in a hotel lobby drinking *alcohol*? It would definitely be misunderstood. Then she told herself that she was tired of all the continual misunderstandings. She was tired after a long day in the office, she was disappointed that her friend was obviously not going to show up for her workshop, and she was going to have her beer: misunderstanding or not. By this time, she was already sitting by a table.

'Esi!' a voiced called out above the steady hum of voices. It was deep and feminine.

'Opokuya!' Esi screamed back, even before looking for the direction from which the voice had come. They were hugging.

They had missed each other, those two friends. They always did even when they were away from one another for only a few days.

And this time they had not been in touch for weeks. Besides, until recently they had lived in different parts of the country for several years. But then they were aware that as two women, each of whom had a demanding career, a husband, a child for one and four children for the other, there was a limit to how much time they could spend together. In any case, what was between them was so firm, so deeply rooted, it didn't demand any forced or even conscious tending. Each of them had realised over the years that perhaps they had managed to stay so close because they made so few demands of one another. Especially in terms of time to idle and gossip. However, whenever it had become necessary to be in daily communication they had done that too, without either of them fussing.

In the lobby other voices bubbled as though in a boiling cauldron, mixing with the clinking of glasses, the steps of men and women coming in and going out, some popular music that intruded subtly from one of the hotel's bars: high life, Afro, rock, Afro beat . . . funk, whatever. In the distance, and from a neo-colonial African city that had barely managed to drag itself through one more weekday, the tired traffic hummed and crawled itself home for the barest of evening meals and a humid tropical night.

Esi and Opokuya talked excitedly, each asking questions of the other and not having time to pause to answer the other's. At the beginning of that chance meeting they were both too pleasantly surprised for the difference in their voice timbres to be noticeable. However, as they settled down, it became clear that Esi's voice was quick and thin – 'silvery' to those who liked her, 'shrill' to those who didn't. Opokuya's voice was slow, low, and a little husky.

Hi, how are you? I am well, and you? How are you? Can't complain. How are the children? They are fine. And those in boarding, have you seen them lately, and how are they? And our little daughter, how is she? Oh, she is fine. You have been hiding! No, it's you who've been hiding . . .

And they went on and on until, tired with the sheer exuberance of their meeting, Esi remembered she had sat down to have a drink just before Opokuya came. When she asked Opokuya whether she could join her at her table, Opokuya said, 'Sure,' and they moved

33

to Esi's table. And the questions and exclamations resumed. Esi wanted to know about Kubi. Was he all right? Opokuya assured her that he was, but then he didn't like Accra or any city much, and so had been complaining endlessly since they got transferred. A note of wistfulness had crept into Opokuya's voice which had not escaped Esi.

'And you?'

'Oh, I am all right,' Opokuya answered quickly.

Almost compelled to console her friend, Esi said she didn't blame Kubi for not caring for 'these urban areas'.

Rather startled by the declaration, Opokuya looked quickly at her friend, 'You know I love cities,' she said pointedly. At that, Esi just laughed.

'This is Opokuya all over again. How can anyone like any of these cities and not feel ashamed to confess it to even a good friend?'

They spent some time ordering things to drink and updating one another on their lives. Esi had a beer and Opokuya had tea. Esi had wanted to stand Opokuya 'a proper drink'. But Opokuya would not hear of it. She insisted that alcohol relaxed her so much that if she took so much as a sip of anything alcoholic, the first thing she would want to do even that early in the evening would be to look for her bed.

'So what?'

Opokuya was shocked.

'But Esi, that would not do at all,' she protested. How could she, Opokuya Dakwa, sleep anytime she felt like it? With a fully grown man, a young growing woman and three growing boisterous boys to feed?

'But you have got some house help, no?' Esi said at one point, in an obvious attempt to convince her friend that she had been listening. But she knew she was not concentrating much.

'Yes,' Opokuya tried to answer, taking the bait, 'in spite of that though, the children and their father refuse to organise even their already-cooked supper when I'm around . . . You'd think that with me being away on duty at such odd hours they would have taught themselves some self-reliance. But no. When I'm home, they try to squeeze me dry to make up for all the times they have to do without me.'

34

Esi laughed again, watching her plump, smooth-skinned, shining-haired friend, and thinking that if that's how people who are squeezed dry normally look, then long live the 'dry-squeeze'.

After a while, both women sighed, declared it was hard all around. But then when Esi suggested that she thought that at least Opokuya should find life a little worthwhile, Opokuya glared at her and demanded why Esi thought so.

'At least, you have got a full life. You have been able to keep your marriage, look at your four wonderful kids.'

'Yes, and my job,' Opokuya added cynically. 'Well, see how ragged I have become in the process of having "a full life".'

'You vain creature! In fact, you look very well and prosperous.' Esi was laughing again, and scolding her friend at the same time.

Presently Opokuya startled Esi with a declaration that she thought Esi was sad. Esi pretended to be puzzled.

'Sad?'

Opokuya conceded that maybe 'sad' was not exactly how Esi's mood could be described but she, Opokuya, was convinced that something was wrong. She knew her friend. There had been a persistent light-heartedness about Esi throughout the years they were growing up: a certain what people described as 'I don't careism' which was also part of her particular charm. Therefore, any diminishing of that spirit got immediately noticed by anyone who knew her well enough. In the meantime, she herself was thinking that it was just like Opokuya to have caught her out so quickly. The fact was that she could not remember feeling so low in a very long time. The last few months had been too 'negatively eventful', as one of her colleagues would say and then go right on to add that:

> One thing Ghanaians are good at is simply turning English down on its head!'

A waiter brought them their orders, and while Esi swallowed large gulps of her beer, Opokuya took rapid sips of her tea, almost as if she was afraid that leaving it standing for a second would cool it beyond rescue.

'You and your hot tea,' Esi teased her kindly.

'Well, you know what my life is. How would I cope without tea, eh?'

'You, Opokuya, cope?' Esi thought she hadn't ever heard anything so ridiculous before. 'You know you would cope in any situation, tea or no tea.'

'I'll ignore that. Maybe in the eyes of a loyal friend I look "prosperous",' she added a little bitterly. Esi opened her mouth to say something. Opokuya stopped her and just went on to remind her that, 'The days when being fat was a sign of prosperity and contentment are long over. You and I know that these days the only fat people in the world are poor uneducated women in the so-called Third World and unhappy sex-starved women in the more affluent societies who are supposed to eat for consolation.'

By the time Opokuya had finished her speech, Esi was laughing so much her eyes were swimming in unshed tears.

'But, Esi, why did you say that at least I've kept my marriage? What's wrong with yours?'

The question was unexpected but should not have been. Esi paused for the minutest moment, then she said rather quietly, 'Opokuya, I have left Oko.'

It was like the booming of a cannon into the evening.

'Esi, what do you mean?'

'Just that. I have left him.'

Absolutely unsure of how to handle the moment, Opokuya seized on the banal: 'How can you leave him? After all, he has been living with you in your bungalow.'

'Opokuya, don't be funny. You know that leaving a man does not always mean that it's the woman who has to get out of the house.'

'I don't know anything. So how did you leave Oko?'

Esi was surprised by how much had happened in the month or so since that Monday when, following their latest argument, Oko had jumped on her. She decided to feel assaulted and from then on, her mind had seized on the 'assault', and held it. Part of its fascination for her was its legal usefulness. She was clever enough to know, if only subconsciously at that stage, that it could come in handy should she ever decide to apply for a proper divorce. Meanwhile, from the evening of that same day, Oko had done all he could to get her to see that, in fact, he had 'jumped on her' because he loved her and that it had been part of his decision to give the relationship a second chance. Esi had not only refused to be convinced, but had in fact got angrier and angrier the harder he had tried to explain. In any case, she had not thought it necessary in the days that followed to change the decision to leave him. Of course, she was aware that although the incident was not the only cause of her disaffection, it had helped her to make up her mind.

'Esi, I'm so sorry,' Opokuya cut into Esi's thoughts.

'Why? Opoku, that marriage was not working . . .'

'Esi, I'm so sorry . . . so sorry.'

They were quiet for a while, then they started to ask about one another's children. Esi wanted to know where Opokuya's children were in school and what they were doing. And Opokuya wanted to know about Ogyaanowa. According to both mothers, all the children were fine, and Ogyaanowa was at Oko's mother's.

'Permanently?'

'Oh no, only until the end of August. Then she'll come back to me for the re-opening of school.'

'How old is she?'

'Six. She is in Primary One this year.'

'Already? But of course, she was born about the time I had my last born, no?'

'Yes.'

'Time does fly.'

'It does.'

The sadness that had descended on them was not proving easy to get rid of. They even went back to what they should have tried to find out from one another when they first met at the hotel: what they were doing here at the Hotel Twentieth Century. Esi told Opokuya about the friend she was supposed to be meeting from abroad, and Opokuya told Esi about the arrangement for Kubi to collect her from the hotel.

'So you and your husband have taken to dropping into the Twentieth Century for drinks?' Esi made a great attempt to tease Opokuya.

Opokuya went on to tell Esi about the trip she was planning to her mother's.

'Homesick?' Esi asked, trying hard to keep her teasing tone.

'Yes.' Opokuya answered, too enthusiastically, and fell into Esi's trap.

'Oh Opoku, shame on you. At your age!'

'Now you stop it. I miss my mother. You know I haven't seen her for a long time.'

'I didn't know.'

'And I miss the feeling of being special with someone.'

'You are very special with Kubi.'

'Esi, you were very special with Oko.'

Esi did not know how to answer that. In the silence that followed, each woman was thinking that clearly the best husband always seems to be the one some other woman is living with!

The sadness returned, heavier than before.

One reason why Esi was almost tongue-tied was that she was too aware that Opokuya was her last hope of gaining understanding or at least some sympathy for her point of view. So far, nobody to whom she had tried to state her case had been remotely sympathetic. Like her mother and her grandmother. She had driven home one Sunday morning to discuss the whole business with them. They had found it very hard to listen to her at all. Although they had tried. When Nana's patience had been stretched beyond endurance, she had asked Esi to tell her truthfully whether the problem was that her husband beat her.

'No, Nana.'

'So, does your husband smell? His body? His mouth?'

Esi couldn't help laughing. 'No, Nana. In fact, for a man, he is very clean, very orderly.'

'So then . . . Listen, does he deny you money, expecting you to use your earnings to keep the house, feed him and clothe him too?'

'Nana, we are not rich. But money is not a big problem.'

'What is the problem?' both her grandmother and her mother really screamed this time: the former with her walking stick raised as though to strike her, and the latter bursting into tears.

Esi had to tell the truth. Her husband wanted too much of her and her time. No, it was not another woman. In fact, she thought she might have welcomed that even more.

'Are you mad?' The older women looked at Esi and she looked at them. How could she tell them she did not want Oko? Where was she going to get a man like him again? At the end of the discussion, her grandmother had told her the matter sounded too much for her ears: she didn't want to hear any more of it. At least not for some time. The declaration was accompanied by a proper palm-rubbing gesture. Finally, as Esi got into her car to drive back to Accra, and almost for a farewell, her mother had called her a fool. She had driven to Accra feeling like one.

As for Oko's people, there never was a question of Esi talking to them. She was convinced they hated her. She knew that for some time his aunts had been trying to get him a woman, 'a proper wife'. What had discouraged them was his lack of enthusiasm and the fact that they suspected Esi didn't care one way or another. The purpose of the project had been two-fold: to get him to make more children, 'because his lady-wife appeared to be very satisfied with only one child,

a terrible mistake, a dangerous situation.'

They also wanted to hurt Esi: very badly, if they could. And if she didn't care one way or another, then there was no point to it, was there? As far as Esi was concerned, his sisters were no better. They used to come and insinuate that their brother was failing in his duties to the family because she had turned his head – with 'something'.

'She fried it with the breakfast eggs!'

'She put it into cakes!'

And they would whisper and laugh. As far as the sisters were concerned, Oko never had money to spend on them because he was busy wasting his salary on her. When Esi let it be known that in fact she earned more than he did, their new line of attack was that it served him right, marrying a woman who had more money than him. His wife could never respect him. It was also around this time that the hints began to drop here and there: about the need for him to get himself an unspoilt young woman, properly brought up, whose eyes have not jumped over her eyebrows with too much education and too much money of her own . . . No she couldn't go to them.

As a result of Esi's growing uncertainty about the justification of her decision, she was hesitating to tell Opokuya her story. And since any hesitation with communication was itself a new development in their relationship, it too was creating its own nervous tensions in her. If Opokuya was her last hope of getting an understanding at all, then she had better not let go of her. For here, where no one ever made the mistake of thinking that any marriage was strictly the affair of the two people involved, one could never attempt to fight any war in a marriage alone. And if she lost Opokuya too, she would have to fight alone.

Before Opokuya moved into Accra recently, she and Esi had only once before lived in the same town since they were in secondary school. It was when Esi and Oko were first married and Esi returned with Oko to Kumasi, where he had been teaching. Kubi was then an assistant surveyor, and Opokuya was still a midwife at the Central Hospital. At the time, neither of them had any marital problems to share. Of course Opokuya as usual had sounded as if she had plenty. But then, as some of her colleagues always said unkindly, Opokuya searched for problems to talk about, so that she too would sound just like any other wife. As for Esi, she was then expecting her baby, and was too recently married to be aware of problems even if there had been any.

After her baby was born, Esi had wanted to return to work. But that had not been easy. She had had to face the difficulty of having to choose between two not so attractive options. She could stay on at Kumasi, but that meant that she would not be working at all, or not meaningfully. It was not every government department that had regional branches. The Department of Urban Statistics was one of those that didn't. Or she could return to Accra for her regular job: as long as she first convinced Oko that they could still see one another as often as possible at weekends, either she going or he coming. But at the merest hint of that, Oko had made it clear that the subject wasn't even up for discussion. He made it clear that as far as he was concerned they had done enough of that kind of travelling when they were 'just friends'. In fact he had thought one reason why they had got married was to give themselves the chance to be together properly, no?

In the end the only option left her, which she had had to take, was to ask to be seconded to the regional census co-ordinating office. She had ended up keeping the Birth and Death register.

'Surely, one doesn't need a Master's degree in statistics to do that?' she would fume and rage daily. Oko ignored her complaints. The truth was that he didn't feel that sympathetic. And neither did the men in the office. In fact, they let her know that she was unwelcome, and a burden they did not know what to do with.

Having to deal with a man who is over-qualified for a job is bad enough.

To have to cope with an over-qualified woman in any situation is a complete misfortune.

Now six years later, both she and Opokuya were here in Accra, working. And she had a marital problem. A big problem. She should just gather herself together, and tell Opokuya what she felt. If Opokuya too could not understand her, then that was that. She would accept that she was just a fool, like her mother and her grandmother had said.

After all, people change. Look at her. Esi had changed. If she now found Oko's attentions so suffocating that she wanted very badly to split, then people change. There was a time when she had been made to fear that in fact she would never marry.

'You have waited too long,' Esi's mother had complained. 'Given your structure, you shouldn't have.' (The poor woman shared the popularly held belief that a young woman who is too tall, too thin, and has flat belly and a flat behind has a slim chance of bearing children. The longer she waits after puberty, the slimmer those chances get!)

Esi's main problem was that she was easily bored. And no woman ever caught a man or held him by showing lack of interest. Esi had known that she would have to work up some enthusiasm in her relationship with men. 'But how?' she had kept asking herself. Now looking back she didn't dare admit, even to herself, that perhaps what she had felt for Oko in the first years of their married life was gratitude more than anything else. Gratitude that in spite of herself he had persisted in courting her and marrying her.

'Not many women are this lucky . . .' Esi could hear her grandmother's voice. 'And who told you that feeling grateful to a man is not enough reason to marry him? My lady, the world would die of surprise if every woman openly confessed the true reasons why she married a certain man. These days, young people don't seem to know why they marry or should marry.'

'What are some of the reasons, Nana?'

'Ah, so you want to know? Esi we know that we all marry to have children . . .'

'But Nana, that is such an old and worn-out idea! Children can be born to people who are not married.'

'Sure, sure, but to help them grow up well, children need homes with walls, a roof, fire, pots.'

'Oh Nana. But one person can provide all these things these days for a growing child!'

'Maybe . . . yes . . . Yes, my lady. We also marry to increase the number of people with whom we can share the joys and the pains of this life.'

'Nana, how about love?'

'Love? . . . Love? . . . Love is not safe, my lady Silk, love is dangerous. It is deceitfully sweet like the wine from a fresh palm tree at dawn. Love is fine for singing about and love songs are good to listen to, sometimes even to dance to. But when we need to count on human strength, and when we have to count pennies for food for our stomachs and clothes for our backs, love is nothing. Ah my lady, the last man any woman should think of marrying is the man she loves.'

6

It was night in Accra. It was not as hot as it had been in the day, but it was still hot, and the atmosphere was heavy with the moisture from the gulf. The Hotel Twentieth Century was blazing with light, consuming enough electricity to light up the whole of the nearby fishing district. But the fishing villages did not have electricity. In fact, all that the fishing community knew of that facility were the huge pylons that stood in their vegetable patches, and the massive cables passing over the roofs of their homes as these bore the electricity to the more deserving members of society. Like users of hotel lobbies. Like Mrs Esi Sekyi and her friend, Mrs Opokuya Dakwa.

Kubi had not shown up yet, and the two women had long stopped expecting him. In fact, they had decided that their chance meeting, along with his failure to be there on time, was a definite advantage. In spite of the long pauses, they were having an old-fashioned relaxed chat, and Esi could always take Opokuya home anyway. However, Opokuya was feeling a little uneasy even though she had long ago taught herself to see her husband as a grown-up person who was perfectly capable of looking after himself; and also that people being late does not always mean they are bleeding to death by some roadside. 'But sometimes they are,' screamed the nurse in her. Maybe she had worked too long in hospitals.

'Esi, exactly what is the problem?' Opokuya couldn't help putting it in her blunt way this time. 'Is it another woman?' As Esi opened her mouth to answer she was also wondering how Opokuya could speak with her grandmother's voice.

'Opokuya, do you remember when you were still up north,

and I stopped at yours for the weekend on my way back from Ouga?'

'You had been on some Ghana–Burkina joint commission, no?'

'Yes.'

'Yes.'

'I had told you then that I was already beginning to feel fed up.'

'Yes, Esi. But why? Is it other women?' Opokuya hated to, but couldn't prevent herself from repeating the question.

> In any case, everyone knows that a man's relationship with women other than his wife, however innocent, can always help ruin a marriage. And that includes his love for his own mother.

'Oh no. To be fair to old Oko, it was never that. In fact sometimes, I wished he would behave like other men in that respect.'

'Esi you are mad.' Opokuya truly couldn't believe her ears.

'That is what my mother and my grandmother said.'

'How many women wouldn't give everything they've got to have a man like that?'

'Well, they can all have him.'

'Listen my sister, you have to be realistic.'

'About what?'

'About life!'

'It's he who wasn't being realistic.'

'No?'

'Well . . . well . . . here we are, two people, each with a demanding job . . .' Opokuya was surprised. Esi was beginning to sound childish and petulant. She had a strong urge to scream at her to stop her story. But that she knew would be unfair. 'Esi, what about your job?'

'As you know, my job can be very demanding sometimes. I have to prepare materials for ministers, permanent secretaries . . . you know, such people. And then I have to do a lot of travelling; inside the country, outside. Oko resented every minute he was free and I couldn't be with him.'

'But that is so natural.'

'For whom?'

'My sister, if a man loves a woman, he would want to have her around as much as possible.'

'To the extent that he would want me to change my job because he thought it took me away from him?'

'Yes,' said Opokuya, wondering where she had acquired such ideas from, and the confidence to express them so forcefully. 'To the extent that he would want you to change your job.'

'But when we first met, Oko told me that what had attracted him most about me was my air of independence!'

Opokuya had begun to giggle, and then discovered she could hardly stop. 'You see, it happens to all of us. Esi, listen: men are not really interested in a woman's independence or her intelligence. The few who claim they like intelligent and active women are also interested in having such women permanently in their beds and in their kitchens.'

'Which is impossible. It's a contradiction.'

'Yes. But there it is. Very few men realise that the sharp girls they meet and fall in love with are sharp because, among other things, they've got challenging jobs in stimulating places. That such jobs are also demanding. That these are also the kinds of jobs that keep the mind active – alive. Look, quite often, the first thing a man who marries a woman mainly for the quickness of her brain tries to do is get her to change her job to a more "reasonable" one. Or to a part-time, not a full-time job. The pattern never, never changes. And then a "reasonable" job is often quite dull too.'

'And no part-time job has the stimulation that its full-time version can give.'

'Exactly! So that when a woman changes jobs in such a manner, more likely than not, her vision begins to shrink, and she begins to get bored and dissatisfied.'

'And even he might begin to find her dull.'

'Sure.'

Swiftly Esi had become aware of a certain desolation moving towards her from far away.

'It's an impossible situation,' she said rather heavily

'It is,' Opokuya agreed, with equal cheerlessness. For a time, they were quiet, Opokuya stirring the cold ghost of her tea, and Esi twirling around her empty glass.

'Let's have another drink,' they both said, at the same time.

They ordered a second beer for Esi, and this time, a gin and lime for
Opokuya, looking with a mischievous understanding at one
another.

'Surely, Kubi is different,' Esi picked up the thread of their
conversation from where they had left it before their drinks came.

'How little you know my husband,' Opokuya declared, not
really wanting to say more.

'He's always seemed so reasonable.'

'Well, go on thinking that. I don't want to disillusion you . . . But
Esi, what are you going to do?'

'About what?'

'Esi, you can't stay alone forever?'

'Why not?'

'It's just not healthy.'

'Says the local representative of the SWI.'

'And what's that?'

Esi was giggling. 'It means Satisfied Wives International. It's
how another girlfriend refers to you all.'

'All of us who?'

'All of you happily married women who are always saying that
being single is not healthy.'

'Oh really?' She hadn't thought of herself as either 'a happily
married woman' or that she belonged to a club of such characters.
Now they were both laughing. 'Actually, I don't know . . . I
thought . . .'

'Don't think,' said Esi, rather sharply, 'especially if your
thoughts are in the region of me going back to Oko.' She took a big
gulp of her beer rather sulkily.

Opokuya stayed quiet for a while before saying seriously that in
fact that was what would normally be expected of her as a good
friend. 'In any case, what are you planning? A proper divorce
soon? A remarriage?' She tried not to sound like a stern busybody.

Esi was vehement: 'Me? Never!'

'Why ever not?'

'I could not bear it,' exclaimed Esi, quite obviously having a
problem keeping her voice down. 'Another husband to sit on my
back all twenty-four hours of the day? The same arguments about
where a woman's place is? Another husband to whine all day about

46

how I love my work more than him? Ugh, Opokuya, I couldn't.
And thank you very much.'

'So back to my question, and forgive me for harassing you, but
Esi, what are you going to do now? After all, you are human. You
must get lonely sometimes?'

'You are not harassing me. Besides, who else do I have who
would discuss things so openly and patiently with me? I'm
definitely human and I most certainly feel lonely sometimes.
Often. But what can I do about it?'

'Really, why throw away a perfectly good husband for the
loneliness of a single woman's life?'

'Opokuya, please don't you also treat me like a child. Just a little
while ago, when I said that I had always thought Kubi was a good
husband, you nicely shut me up. It is beginning to look as if the
nicest husband is always the one someone else is living with, no?'
And each of them was shocked that the thought had finally become
words.

'Say that again, my sister,' agreed Opokuya. 'But mind you,' she
thought she should seize the calmness in the discussion at that
point, and press home an idea, 'unlike so many cities abroad, there
isn't much here that a single woman can do to relieve the loneliness
and boredom of the long hours between the end of the working day
and sleep.'

'You mean when a single woman is actually living alone?'
'Yes.'

'You can say that again. It is even more frightening to think that
our societies do not admit that single women exist. Yet . . .'

'Yet what?'

'Single women have always existed here too,' she said with some
wonder.

'Oh yes. And all over the continent . . .'

'Women who never managed to marry early enough.'

'Or at all. Widows, divorcees.'

'I wonder what happened to such women.'

'Like what?'

'Think about it carefully.'

'I am sure that as usual, they were branded witches.' Esi said,
laughing.

'Don't laugh Esi, it's serious. You may be right. Because it is easy to see that our societies have had no patience with the unmarried woman. People thought her single state was an insult to the glorious manhood of our men. So they put as much pressure as possible on her –'

'– until she gave in and married or remarried, or went back to her former husband.'

'And of course if nothing cured her they ostracised her and drove her crazy.'

'And then soon enough, she died of shame, loneliness and heartbreak.'

At this point, both Esi and Opokuya burst out laughing again. Almost hysterically. As they calmed down Opokuya said, 'Esi, it's not funny,' and Esi said, 'Opokuya, it's not funny.'

'But Opokuya,' Esi resumed the discussion, 'how come you know so much about these problems? After all you've been happily married all your adult life.'

'Happily married, eh? I'll let that too pass. Have you forgotten that I have been a nurse and midwife over the period under discussion? Esi, in that profession, with that kind of specialisation, no one can prevent herself from learning about women and human beings generally. In fact, people oppress you with information. And what they don't tell you, you easily stumble on.'

'Oh yes, I see what you mean . . . Opokuya, what can I do?'

'Ah-h-h! Now listen to who is asking what!' Opokuya was enjoying her triumph.

'Please be serious.'

'I am always serious . . . What do you think you can do?'

'There was a problem lying in the bush,

'You went and dragged it into your house.'

Esi could hear her grandmother singing. Then, almost to herself, 'I'm sure there'll be no solution for me. Unless I meet a man who is prepared to accept my lifestyle.'

'Your lifestyle? Esi, if you continue in that way, you will get into trouble. Because, my dear, no man is totally going to accept your lifestyle.'

'So what do I do with my loneliness?'

'You don't know what loneliness is.'

'Opoku . . .'

'Ah, but you. Did you really think you were lonely? My sister, you don't know. What I was going to say though is that, if you really were lonely, and you wanted to do something about it badly enough, you would know what to do.'

'What do you mean?'

'Ah. I thought you people who go to universities know and understand everything.'

'Now you are being nasty.'

'Forgive me, my sister. I didn't mean it like that.'

'So what was all that leading to?'

'Simple. You just can't have everything your way, and not expect to be lonely, at least some of the time.'

After that, they both fell silent for a while.

'No, you can't, Esi,' Opokuya said, as if there had been no pause. 'No matter what anybody says, we can't have it all. Not if you are a woman. Not yet.'

'Our society doesn't allow it.'

'Esi, no society on this earth allows that.'

'Oh Lord.'

'I know I'm beginning to sound disagreeable. But I thought it was clear that whatever other faults he may have, which of course I wouldn't know about, Oko loved you and wanted your marriage to work.'

'On his terms.'

'It had to be on someone's terms.'

'Why not on mine?'

'Why are you now being so childish, eh? Our people have said that for any marriage to work, one party has to be a fool.'

'And they really mean the woman, no?'

'Naturally.'

They both burst out laughing again.

'I knew it,' exclaimed Esi.

'That's how life is.'

'Well, I'm having none of it. P-e-r-i-o-d.'

'Esi, if you really looked around at the world of husbands, wouldn't you admit that Oko wasn't that bad?' Then almost laughing again, 'You should have tried harder to squeeze out some time for him.'

'How? How could I have done more than I did as a wife and a mother, and still be able to compete on an equal basis with my male colleagues in terms of my output? How can I do more than I'm already doing and compete effectively for promotion, travel opportunities and other side-benefits of the job?'

Opokuya couldn't contain her patience any longer: 'Esi, Esi, Esi! . . . What kind of talk is this? Ah. So you gave extra time to your job. You did the necessary travelling and attended the necessary conferences. You competed effectively and got promoted. Now look at what has happened to your marriage. Where does that leave you?'

They fell into another trough of silence, because they had both been mildly shocked by Opokuya's outburst. Opokuya herself was wondering what had gotten into her, and hadn't she gone too far? Esi was thinking that she didn't know Opokuya cared that much, and could Opokuya – and therefore everybody else – be right and she wrong? And in spite of her doubts, Opokuya couldn't keep quiet anyway.

'Your male colleagues have still got their wives?' she said almost angrily.

'Not to mention the odd girlfriend or two,' Esi added.

'I'm glad you realise that yourself, eh? And of course their wives and girlfriends are still waiting for them to come back home from more conferences . . . And where is your husband?'

There was another long silence. Then Esi spoke.

'Opokuya, I don't think I'm beginning to regret anything. But in fact, considering how much I put in my job . . . sometimes I even take home data to analyse! I never get that much from it, not half as much as those men . . . and even with the promotion, they passed me over a couple of times . . .'

'Now, stop. How do you know I want to hear all of that?'

'Why is life so hard on the professional African woman?' Esi asked, her voice showing that she was a little puzzled.

But Opokuya wasn't having any of her self-pity. So she countered rather heavily. 'Why is life so hard on the non-professional African woman? Eh? Esi, isn't life even harder for the poor rural and urban African woman?'

'I think life is just hard on women,' Esi agreed, trying to calm Opokuya down.

'But remember it is always harder for some other women somewhere else,' Opokuya insisted. Both of them sighed.

Esi opened her mouth to say something, then she clapped it quickly shut, opened her eyes wide and exclaimed in a whisper, 'Opokuya, look who is here!'

'Who . . . who?' Opokuya asked, looking frantically around. But of course, there was no way she could easily have spotted the object of Esi's excited attention, since she hadn't met him before. Esi on her part was following him with her eyes as he, just as she had earlier, went straight up to the front desk. She tried not to stare too hard. But there was no doubt that she was interested in whoever he was. Finally, Opokuya said, with something like awe in her voice, 'You mean that one?'

'Yes.'

'Do you know him?'

'Yes. That's Ali. Kondey. Ali Kondey.'

Ali too had seen Esi the moment he entered the lobby. And although he had gone to the reception truly to make inquiries about a business associate he was expecting, he was also conscious of the need for him to use that time to recover from the extreme agitation that had attacked him at the sight of Esi. Then he was walking towards where the two friends were sitting.

As he got nearer their table, he extended his right arm. 'A-llo, Esi.'

'Hello, Ali,' said Esi, somewhat tremulously.

'How nice to see you.'

'I thought you were out of the country.'

'Actually, since we last met, I've been in and out more than once.'

'You are hardly a resident here.'

'I know, it's the fault of my job.'

Both of them suddenly remembered that Opokuya was around.

'Oh, Ali, meet my friend Mrs Opokuya Dakwa. Opoku, Mr Ali Kondey.'

'Hello, Mr Kondey.'

51

'Hello.'

Esi came back to Ali, 'Would you like to join us?'

Much of Ali's charm poured out. 'You know I would love to,' he said, 'but I've got a guest here from across the border, and we are having a little conference in his room. In fact, I just spoke to him from the desk. He is expecting me.'

'That's okay then,' Esi squeaked, her voice gone even thinner.

'Still, it is a shame I can't join you,' Ali added. 'But could I please phone you sometime during the coming week, Esi?'

Esi said that that would be fine. Ali thanked her, adding that it was a pleasure meeting Opokuya. Then he was gone.

'God, he is gorgeous,' breathed Opokuya, as soon as she was sure Ali wouldn't hear her.

Esi agreed that Ali was handsome. Then with enormous surprise, Opokuya noticed that Esi's eyes were sparkling. She stayed quiet for a fraction of a second, and then asked Esi easily if she did not know Ali Kondey rather well.

'Sort of,' Esi said, not so easily.

'So what is this rubbish lonely-hearts line you've been serving me? And there was idiot me trying so hard to console you. Hah! Hah! Hah!' Opokuya had pretended to be angry and ended up laughing. Esi giggled.

'Please, Opoku.'

'Please my foot. I just caught you out. That's all.'

'You see, it wasn't something I thought I could talk easily about, even to you.'

'No?'

'Not really . . . it's true he's been showing a lot of interest. Bringing me all sorts of gifts from his travels. Stuff like that. But I've been trying not to encourage him.'

'Why not? After all, if you are leaving Oko or you have already left him, then you might as well take an insurance policy.'

'Opoku, you are not being nice. And in any case, you know I'm not at all smart in these things.'

'Esi, I know nothing. In fact, I'm beginning to think I don't know anything about you.'

'Oh, don't say that. Besides, the situation is quite complicated.'

'How? . . . There is a wife?'

'Opoku . . .'

'Ah, but you. Did you really think you were lonely? My sister, you don't know. What I was going to say though is that, if you really were lonely, and you wanted to do something about it badly

Esi sighed rather audibly, 'There is.'

Opokuya heard the sigh, and became immediately concerned, 'You like him, heh?'

'Very very much.'

'I don't blame you. He looks good enough to eat.'

Opokuya suggested it really was time they went home. Esi agreed. Just as she had expected, Opokuya was feeling a little drowsy after the alcohol, and more than a little uneasy about her husband and the fact that she'd been away from her home for so long, and unexpectedly. Besides, both she and Esi were tired from the intensity of the discussion. They beckoned the waiter who had been serving them throughout the evening, and when he came, they asked for their bill. After they had settled that, they picked up their handbags, went out of the hotel lobby and into Esi's car.

In the end, they never managed to leave the hotel together. Opokuya saw Kubi long before he saw her. She followed their vehicle with her eyes, as he pulled in looking for parking space. When she asked Esi to stop, Esi wouldn't switch off the engine.

'Why are you in such a hurry? Stay and say hello to Kubi.'

'No,' said Esi, almost in a panic.

'You think he'll quiz you about Oko?' She had read Esi's mind.

'Yes,' it was another confession. 'And I couldn't go through with it, not now.'

Opokuya thought they should both meet Kubi so that Esi could say a quick hello. It would make it easier for her to explain how she had managed to spend an entire evening at the hotel, although the fact that she had had to was not even her fault. Almost immediately, they saw him driving towards them. Opokuya moved quickly and went to stand in the vehicle's path. Kubi screeched to a stop.

'Opokuya, you scared me!' Kubi protested to a laughing Opokuya.

'You must stop playing dangerous and childish games.'

'Hello Kubi,' said Esi to a very surprised Kubi. He returned the greeting. But before he knew what was happening, Esi had said something like, 'See you, Opokuya,' and just gone off.

Kubi remembered that there were other cars behind him, so he moved the car forward.

'I'm very sorry,' Kubi offered in response to a question Opokuya had not asked aloud. 'And in any case, I had told you this morning that we were going to have a meeting. These days, you should know how these budgetary meetings are.'

'A reference to my new position at the hospital, no doubt?'

'Well, why not?'

Opokuya decided that getting angry wouldn't do any good. But she still could not help asking whether his budgetary meeting had really gone on until nearly nine o'clock in the evening.

'No, not really. But it was still quite late when we finally finished – maybe around seven – and I had thought by then you would have found your way home . . .' There was no doubt that now his voice was asking a question.

'Actually, Esi and I bumped into one another, so we sat and had a chat. I kept hoping that sooner or later, you would come . . .'

Kubi thought he had better not say what he was going to say. That surely Esi too had a husband and a child, and shouldn't she have tried to go home earlier to take care of her household? They were both silent all the way home; which was extremely frustrating for both of them. Kubi had been looking forward all evening to asking Opokuya about her time with his sister – as an excuse to voice more boldly his objection to her proposed trip to her mother's.

Opokuya too had looked forward to telling him about her time with his sister. How Connie had assured her that 'all would be fine for the kids to come . . . of course. And anyway, what is this business of coming all the way here just to ask whether the children could stay with me while you are away? Isn't my house their home . . .? You shouldn't worry about a thing. You can go away whenever it is convenient for you.'

She had also wanted to tell Kubi the latest news about Esi and Oko. Somewhat uncertainly this time. She knew Kubi wouldn't like that. Although their friendship was older than their marriage, she and Esi had also been lucky to have married men who got on rather well, and genuinely liked one another's wife. In fact, because Esi was still in the university when Opokuya and Kubi got married, Kubi had always treated Esi more or less like a younger sister, with openly demonstrated affection. So that if Opokuya hadn't been such a confident woman she would have found it difficult not to be jealous of the relationship between her husband and her friend. Not to mention the fact that Esi and Kubi spoke the same language. Opokuya's first language was supposed to be only a dialect of the same language. But the version in their part of the country had lost or rather gained from its contact with the majority language of that region. So it had become a little foreign. When Esi and Kubi spoke she understood a whole lot. But it was never enough to enable her to catch the nuances behind their words – especially when they spoke fast. However, she had long ago told herself that she already had enough problems to cope with. What would happen to her if she started suspecting her husband and her best and only real friend? Such things happened of course. But Esi and Kubi?

Having sorted that out with herself, life had in fact been quite easy. She was able to enjoy both her friend and her husband, content to leave each day to take care of its unpredictable self, as far as 'all that' was concerned.

Opokuya's decision to trust her husband had paid off in other ways. She never let herself worry about Kubi's chronic lateness; whether it had to do with normal office affairs, or indeed, any kind of affair or affairs. For instance, he could be taking a woman or women with him on his bush trips. She was aware that most men in his position did. Again, she had taken some time to think seriously through it. The only conclusion she had arrived at about that too was that, short of insisting on going with him on every trip, a very silly and unlikely thing for her to do, she would never know the truth. So again she had asked herself, why worry about it?

Opokuya still fretted at Kubi's daily late return from work all the same. But for two completely different reasons. She was anxious for his safety. What would she do if something happened to him? She had lived among his people all her life, from the time she had travelled west to come to boarding school when she was about fourteen years old. Of course, she had gone home every school holiday. But what was a total of four months in a whole year? She had returned to this part of the country in order to go through nursing school, and later to specialise in midwifery. She had met and got married to Kubi. Clearly, she was as good as a stranger in her own part of the country. If anything happened to Kubi, where was she going to go? Nowhere other than where she was, that was clear. She would definitely have to stay in this city, with her children, a native of nowhere. Kubi's people were kind and considerate, but they had not managed to convince her that she was one of them. They couldn't. After all, most people wish their sons and daughters would marry the the girl or boy from next door, or at least from the neighbourhood. And she definitely hadn't been from Kubi's neighbourhood! She knew better than to complain. Some other women in similar situations were much worse off than her . . . and in any case, she would rather not think of anything happening to Kubi. Not just yet, dear Lord.

Of course, the other reason why she fretted daily at Kubi coming home late was the car. That she could never get used to. To have a car parked all those hours when it could have been moving?

As they parked outside the gate of their bungalow, she realised the day was truly over.

I envy Esi's freedom of movement, she thought rather non-consequentially. She also realised suddenly that in fact she had been thinking that for a very long time.

7

Ali and Fusena had been classmates at the post-secondary teacher training college at Atebubu. He had been twenty-three years old then and she twenty-one. From the very first day they set eyes on one another as 'ninos' in their first week on campus, they had taken to each other. At that time, it was not 'like' as in 'lovers', but 'like' as in 'like'. Just good friends they were most of the time, and sometimes a little more like brother and sister. For their three years on campus, they often spent a lot of their free time sharing discoveries, comparing notes and even swotting together.

The college was one of those that had been almost deliberately placed in confluent towns of Ghana to attract aspiring teachers from the dominant ethnic groups in equal proportions. However, on the campus at Atebubu, as on the others, the students still maintained a tendency to relate along ethnic lines. Ali was of course a loner in that respect. He was not a southerner, and he did not feel like a northerner, or an upper either, what with his French accent and all.

But Ali liked the company of interesting women, and right from the beginning he found Fusena very interesting. For instance, most evenings after supper, they would stay together until curfew. The college was co-educational, but the campus was strictly segregated. And 'curfew' was how the students described the hours of the night when according to the rules, men and women students were not to be seen together.

Around this time it never occurred to either Ali or Fusena to admit that there could be much else between them apart from friendship. What indications existed in their separate hearts as to what else could be possible was for each of them a closely guarded secret that was not revealed to their conscious selves. What Ali could not admit even to himself was that he felt jealous anytime he saw Fusena talking to any male other than himself. Whether the male was a teacher or a student made no difference.

Fusena on her part could also not bear to see Ali relate to any woman other than herself. In fact, once when she had gone to his room and met a girl-student there she had become depressed for days. After they graduated, they both went to teach at primary schools in Tamale. So Ali and Fusena continued to see one another regularly. But they were still just good friends. Meanwhile, throughout what was now six years of their friendship, each of them had got involved in a number of love affairs that seemed not to have been given much opportunity to grow.

Fusena had come close to getting married once. The suitor had been an important man in the government with lots of years between him and Fusena, lots of other wives, lots of new money and heavy political power. He was an *alhaji*. As soon as he realised that she was not going to be easy to woo he had set about the business of winning her, as though she too was a parliamentary seat. Apart from carting loads of presents to her house for her mother and father as well as half of her extended family, he had sent around his thugs to warn any man he thought could be interested in Fusena as a lover. And of course that had included Ali. But the latter had been only amused by all the happenings at that time. Surely enough though, one evening he heard a knock on his door, and when he opened it he found a giant on his doorstep and concluded that his messenger had come. He treated the man with great charm and courtesy, so that before the man had even begun the verbal part of his mission, Ali had convinced him that there was no way he, Ali, could be interested in any man–woman relationship with Fusena. Why, Fusena was the sister he had always wanted but never had. Allah, and ordinary mortals too, were his witnesses. He had been worrying himself about the fact that Fusena was not married. In fact, he considered he had failed in his duties that he never managed to get Fusena married to any of the very intelligent male colleagues at the teacher-training college. At this the big man's giant had grunted menacingly. But you see, Ali continued without pausing, maybe Allah knew what he was doing. Clearly, he was preserving Fusena for the *alhaji*. The giant's face exploded in a blinding brightness. As for himself, Ali stressed, he was going to do all that was in his power actually to promote the *alhaji's* cause.

Ali had thought he had been quite earnest at the time. It was only later that he could admit – and always with some panic – that perhaps he had suspected all along that Fusena had had no intention of marrying the man. When she announced that decision, her mother, Mma Abu, nearly lost her mind, for two main reasons. First there were all the riches that had seemed so easily within their grasp, and which they had now lost.

Then there was the bigger question of Fusena and marriage. Mma Abu had thought her friends and relatives were just being jealous when Fusena passed her examinations to go to college. They had tried to stop her from going and had tried to get her to marry. Now everyone was just laughing at her behind her back. A twenty-six-year-old woman not married? Was she ever going to? When?

When Mma Abu accepted that she could not deal with the matter of Fusena and marriage any longer, she went to consult the family *mallam*. The *mallam* read from the Holy Book, threw his cowries, drew his lines, and told her not to worry. Her time would come.

'And sir, when that time comes, would she not be too old to have children?'

The great man threw his head back and laughed. Human beings are so predictable, Allah! 'No,' he replied briefly.

'How many children would she have?'

'Ah, she will surely have the same number of children that Allah gave her from the beginning of time.'

Then the big man *alhaji* had come. Everyone had said that he wanted to marry Fusena because he needed a young and smart wife who would run his new businesses and keep his accounts for him.

So what? Mma Abu thought. No one ever marries just to marry. There is always a special reason. The *alhaji* was making a good choice then, because she had always known that her daughter was clever. 'She can be something of a little fool at times. But then, these days, being foolish is a sickness that so many educated people seem to suffer permanently from. Only Allah knows why . . .'

One morning, Fusena had announced that she was not going to marry the *alhaji*. Allah! Everyone thought she was joking. But whether the madness was her own or something someone had given her, Fusena never changed her mind. Not all Mma Abu's tears or the harshest scoldings from her other mothers could move Fusena. Mma Abu could not deal with the crisis. She went back to the *mallam*. But this time, he didn't bother to throw cowries or draw any lines. He just read from the Holy Book and meditated for a short while. When he looked up he told Mma Abu to be patient. 'Fusena has a husband; when he is ready he will reveal himself.'

'Sir, shall I try to find out who he is from Fusena?'

'No.'

'But sir, . . .'

'Mma Abu, if you ask Fusena about him and she herself does not know him yet what will you do next?' Mma Abu shut her mouth tightly. 'Go. Give some alms to the poor. If there are other problems, come back. But please, forget about Fusena and her marriage.'

In the end it was circumstances that forced Ali and Fusena to face their emotions. Towards the end of their third year of teaching at Tamale, Ali informed Fusena that he had been selected as one of a group from their area for a special scholarship. The central government wanted trained personnel from the region for all sorts of assignments. The scholarships were tenable in England. Overseas. It was good news, definitely. It was also then that they realised this meant a long parting which, privately, neither of them was willing to face.

One evening found them together at Ali's, while he was getting ready to go to Bamako in the morning to tell his family the good news of the scholarship. Suddenly he straightened up and turned to face Fusena fully.

'Fusena?'

'Hmm . . . hmm?'

'Would you be shocked if I asked you to marry me?'

'Yes . . . But I would also say yes.'

Later neither of them could remember just how they managed to get through the next couple of months. Suddenly there were so many things to do and hardly any time at all to do anything in.

Ali had hurried home to give his two pieces of news. And his elders had welcomed both of them. Baba Danjuma who normally was a man of very few words had, for once in his life, made a speech about how he had always known Ali would make good, and how good it is to get the younger generations to marry and settle down.

'Allah be praised. It is one of the few things that make one feel good about this nasty business of having to die.'

Mma had disapproved of that statement. 'Baba Danjuma, so how old is any of us that you should already be talking of our death?'

Ali Baba had intervened on behalf of his brother-in-law, 'But my sister, whether it is today or in another one hundred years' time, die we all must.'

Mma Danjuma had turned to stare at her brother as if he had gone mad. She was on the point of saying something again. Then she had remembered that somehow people always talk of death at marriages, and discuss marriages and other happy events at funerals.

There was no doubt at all that Musa Musa had been extremely pleased at the news that at last Ali had decided to marry. Although for a long time he had made it a point not to let anyone know that, deep down, he was worried over his son's continued bachelorhood. Anytime he had passed through Bamako and Mma had broached the subject, he had laughed and asked her to remember that in fact Ali was much much younger than he himself had been when he married Ali's mother.

'But then how many other women had you already married by the time you were ten years younger than Ali?'

'A-h-h-h, but as Allah and even ordinary people are my witnesses, I was not busy learning all the book knowledge in the world, like Ali is doing.'

And now all the arguments were over. There were only discussions which were almost non-stop and which lasted through the next two nights and two days. At dawn on the third day Mma took the once-a-day bus south to Ghana. Her immediate destination was the old homestead on the border between Burkina Faso, Ghana and Togo. It had been agreed that it would be unforgivable not to let their relatives know of such an important event; and in any case, it would make matters so much easier for Mma to go and commandeer some of those relatives and take them along with her, because they would not only know about Fusena's people, but probably spoke something of their language as well. Besides, it would give Mma the perfect excuse to show her face there without having to put up with too many complaints. For sure, there was going to be the usual recitation about people who travelled and never looked back unless . . . Aha, but then, marriage is not a bad piece of news for any wanderer to bring home, is it? Unlike the 'great unmentionable'. Then Mma told her mind to please stop just there.

Right from the beginning, things had gone quite well with Mma's mission. In the end she had got even more volunteers than she needed. She decided two would be enough. She and her cousins arrived in Tamale early in the afternoon of the second day. They went straight to the home of yet another distant relative, a man who was a well-known transport owner. They had been welcomed warmly and given water to wash their feet and hands, food to eat and somewhere to sleep. Custom demanded that even before the Kondeys revealed themselves to Fusena's people, a great deal of research had to be done. Under normal circumstances such research took time, and a year for it was quite usual. But their circumstances were not at all normal, so they could allow themselves only one day and one night.

In the evening of the travellers' second day in Tamale and Mma's fourth day on the road, the Kondeys went to knock on the door of the Al-Hassans.

Now please don't ask me which Tamale Al-Hassans these were. You know all the Al-Hassans are powerful. I don't like trouble. So even if I knew the particular group who were Fusena's people, I would not say.

So the Kondeys knocked on the door of the Al-Hassans, and they were asked to step across the threshold and enter the compound. When all had sat down and the Kondeys had told their story the Al-Hassans had asked for one year to think about the matter. One

Kondey woman who was not known for her patience whispered rather loudly that perhaps all those Al-Hassans were deaf. Had they not heard anything that they had been told? Including the fact that their son was getting ready to go and learn in far away lands? In a few months? Of course, the woman had meant what she was saying to be completely heard by the Al-Hassans. Which they did. And did they get angry?

'Well, our daughter is not a cow. You cannot negotiate for her in half a day.'

'How much time do you need? Twenty years?'

It almost became a serious fight in the end, although no one was unduly worried about that sort of altercation. After all, the ancients had said that you should worry if things went too smoothly on such an occasion, because it meant that the real storms were waiting ahead for the young couple.

The Al-Hassans wanted three months. The three months were whittled down to one week. Beyond that, they refused to go. Mma Danjuma and her relatives packed up and left.

When they got back to the old homestead, everyone agreed that there was no point in Mma returning to Bamako, that a week was no time at all, and that it would come very soon. Mma stayed. Within the week, she sent a message home to Bamako to say she was fine, that things were moving well and that when she had actually caught the little bird in her trap, they would see her face. The message was understood and well received in Bamako. Meanwhile, Ali had been restless, wanting to return south: first to see Fusena at Tamale and then to Accra to begin to find out and do all that was necessary for the trip abroad. However, he was told to be patient, that it was better that he waited for Mma to return. Then whatever she brought with her would be known to him, and his mind could be at ease on that particular score.

To cut a very long story short and as had been foreseen, the week did not take long to come. It was very early on a *harmattan* morning and the country was cloaked in heavy bridal mists when Mma and her cousins set out from their relatives' house in Tamale to return to the Al-Hassans. Meanwhile the Al-Hassans seemed to have been satisfied with the result of their investigations. In the end, everyone had approved of everything. It was that kind of a union.

'After all,' said somebody to whoever cared to listen, 'these days you have to be careful. Especially when they are both young and have had some white man's education.' ' . . . And they had met already!'

A bare two months after the negotiations, Ali and Fusena had a proper Muslim wedding.

The understanding had been that Fusena would continue teaching at Tamale while Ali went overseas, settled down and sent for her. It was all rather ideal. One thing both families insisted on was that Ali should make sure that Fusena was pregnant before he left the country.

'And why?' he had wondered.

'It's always best,' was all anyone would tell him.

Without being an 'armstrong', Ali had always been careful with money. In fact, he had started to save from even the allowances they had been given as trainee teachers. He had also learned that the scholarship he and the others were going on was quite generous. Then there was Fusena's own salary. Maybe even with him out of the country, Fusena would not find it too difficult to look after herself and a child? Four months after he arrived in England Fusena wrote to confirm that, indeed, she was expecting their first child.

Ali had sailed through his examinations like a fine skiff on a calm sea. He had both his bachelor's and master's degrees in record time. He was away for a total of half-a-dozen years – the first three without Fusena. During that period, Mma Abu never lost an opportunity to remark on how long he had been gone, and whether it was a real marriage Fusena was involved in. Then suddenly a cable had come one day from the south, asking Fusena to go and collect tickets for herself and their son, whom they had named Adam. They left for England.

Ali was at the airport to meet them. That day also bore in itself an unbelievable coincidence. From the airport Ali had taken them to his one-bedroom apartment somewhere in the city of London and immediately rushed back to his university. When he returned home in the evening, his normally dancing eyes were virtually doing acrobatics. He had news. Great news. He had got his degree. Fusena was also beside herself with joy. The next day when he was leaving the apartment he told her to see to it that she had lots of rest.

'Why?'

'We will be going out to celebrate. Your arrival and my degree.'

That made a lot of sense, and that was her Ali. He always did the most charmingly appropriate things. She didn't know it then, but the restaurant to which he had taken her after first seeing a film was one of the best in the city. Ali had told her that it was a Chinese place, and what they offered appeared closer to the food at home than any other foreign foods he had tasted in London.

While they were eating, Fusena asked Ali why he had sent for them just then if he had also finished his studies there.

'To begin with, even if I was going to go back home immediately I would still have liked to have you and Adam here. For a bit of a holiday for you, and maybe some shopping before we all went back together. But I am not going back just yet.'

'Why?'

So Ali told Fusena that after the coup, he and others on the special scholarship had received letters from The Castle telling them that the new government had decided it would not be needing their services. That they should consider the programme they were on cancelled.

'Ei, the coup, Ali!'

'Ah-hah?'

Fusena could hardly speak. According to her, the world at home had turned completely crazy. All over the country the programmes that had been initiated by the old regime were being wound up or sold off to private individuals. And very cheaply: as though they were perishable goods at the end of a market day. Her eyes were full of unshed tears. Ali told Fusena to forget all that, and remember they had gone out to celebrate. But by then, it was clear that more than half their appetites had gone.

Soon after finishing his degree examinations, and even before Fusena arrived, Ali had got a full-time job. And now he began to study part-time for a Master's in Economics and Business Administration. Fusena on the other hand sat at home in their one-bedroom apartment or did her housework and looked through catalogues.

When she went out, it was to shop or to window-shop. Then she became pregnant with the second baby. So from then it was being pregnant, nursing the new baby, looking after Adam and Ali, and staring at London's bleak and wet views.

That was hard: the rain. Fusena kept asking herself how a daughter of the dry savannas of Africa could have ended up in such a rain-soaked hole.

> And yet you would have thought that with her memory
> of perpetual drought, anyone would never get tired of
> waters or rain.

Not Fusena. She did get tired and very quickly too. In those days, London was still very English and marked by an absence of the technological conveniences that were already being taken for granted in North America and much of Europe. Were there at least neighbourhood laundromats? Fusena could not have answered the question. There was none in her neighbourhood. So for her, London was shopping trolleys loaded with baby food and breakfast cereals; nappies steaming around a gas fire. And other permanently wet laundry which you left out in the rain, because there was no point bringing it in with hopes of taking it out again when the sun came out. The sun never shone. As for Fusena's mind, it gradually refused to take in anything heavier than the tabloids with their sex-for-sale and other scandals. Except that she was often too busy to read much of even that.

The rain was not the only problem Fusena had with her life as Ali's wife in London. One rainy day, it occurred to her that life should offer more than marriage. That is, if the life she was leading was in fact marriage. To begin with, she was beginning to admit to herself that by marrying Ali, she had exchanged a friend for a husband. She felt the loss implied in this admission keenly, and her grief was great. The first time that this hit her, she actually sat down and wept bitterly. She also knew immediately that there was nothing she could do about her situation. Leaving Ali was not only impossible but would also not be an answer to anything. Because having married her friend and got a husband, there was no chance of her getting back her friend if she left or divorced Ali the husband. She would only have an estranged husband. Nor did it

66

help matters much that in the middle of all her frustrations, she kept telling herself that given the position of women in society, she would rather be married than not, and rather to Ali than anyone else.

Fusena had stared hard at London and admitted that she had another problem. It was this business of Ali getting more and more educated while she stayed the same. Sometimes she truly felt desperate. For whereas she could console herself that she would leave the wetness of London behind her once they were back home, she knew the other problems would stay with her.

And they did. At the end of their first week back home in Ghana, Fusena knew she was pregnant with their third child. So their first couple of years back home, she was busy being pregnant, nursing another infant, helping Ali to find somewhere for them to live and making a home. By the end of those two years, she could not even remember how it felt to be in a schoolroom. Clearly, to go back to teaching after those years and what they contained was going to be hard enough even if Ali had not kept telling her that it was not really necessary.

'It is a waste of time,' he said. 'The hours are long and the pay is terrible.' He would earn enough to look after all of them. Which he did. But Fusena's dissatisfaction did not go away. After all, like nearly all West African women, she had been brought up in a society that had no patience with a woman who did not work. Her husband's wealth or ability to support her was a matter of only mild importance – just something that could make life easier.

'But, Fusena, teaching is out of the question,' Ali would insist during the regular discussions they had on the issue. 'There should be a more lucrative job you could do and still have time to look after the children.' He bought her a massive kiosk at a strategic site in Accra. They said of it that what Fusena's kiosk did not sell was not available anywhere in the country. And when she heard they were saying that she made more money from the kiosk than the largest supermarket in town, she only smiled to herself.

And now here was Ali telling her that he was thinking of making a woman with a university degree his second wife. So Allah, what was she supposed to say? What was she expected to do?

8

When Ogyaanowa went to stay with her grandmother at the beginning of the long vacation, the understanding had been that she would return home to Esi and Oko for the re-opening of school. However, as the marriage began to fall apart, Oko's mother had become just a little nasty about everything. It had seemed to Esi that the older woman was getting ready to use the child as some sort of a weapon to fight her with, and she had secretly sworn not to let that happen. So one day, and much to her mother-in-law's surprise, she had suggested to her that Ogyaanowa could stay on. 'The bungalow gets too lonely for her. Here, there would be other children for her to play with. Nearly all her cousins . . .'

'Please, don't call them her cousins,' her mother-in-law had reprimanded.

'But . . . but Maa,' Esi had virtually stammered, 'aren't they her cousins?'

'You know that in our custom, there is nothing like that. Oko's sisters' children are Ogyaanowa's sisters and brothers. Are we Europeans that we would want to show divisions among kin?'

Esi had felt completely ashamed. She suspected the older woman was seizing on the issue to put her in her place.

So Ogyaanowa had continued to stay at her grandmother's and get completely spoilt. And it was true, there were lots of other people nearer her own age for her to play with. Esi didn't want to admit that the arrangement suited all parties concerned. But it did. Just like any mother, she found it difficult to accept that her child could be happy in any environment other than the one she had created. However, the truth of the matter was that if

Ogyaanowa had been still at the bungalow, she would have felt at least a little funny bringing in Ali so soon after virtually throwing Oko out.

> Guilt is born in the same hour with pleasure,
> like anything in this universe and its enemy.

Just as earthquakes and floods become landmarks in the history of nations, the morning when Oko jumped on Esi became a landmark in their relationship: referred to thereafter by both of them as 'That Morning'. Well, 'That Morning' had been the first day of the secondary school holidays which was why he was able to linger in bed.

It was now about a year since Esi and Opokuya had met at the lobby of the Hotel Twentieth Century, and nearly fourteen months since That Morning. Oko blamed himself for overstaying in bed. He could not stop thinking that perhaps if he had got himself up at his usual early hour he would later have found a better way to show his determination to give their relationship another chance. It was always possible that some alternative existed which would have been more acceptable to Esi, rather than the one he had chosen which had had such unfortunate repercussions.

Anyway, from That Morning, he had spent a good deal of the long vacation checking up on his new school. After each trip, he had returned with glowing reports. The school was big. The grounds were well kept. Neat. The headmaster's office was impressive. Ah, a real office of his own to work in . . . a lovely bungalow with at least four spacious bedrooms . . . It wouldn't be a bad idea for Esi and Ogyaanowa to get out of the city at the weekend. In fact, as things were working out, with his place and her place, they really had a house in the country and a house in town, no? For two people in public service a rather luxurious prospect, no? Esi had refused to be in any way impressed.

Gradually his enthusiasm began to die down. Esi had thought he didn't know her, but he did. Events of That Morning might have outraged her, but it could not be the whole story. She was just using it. This was the point from which he had begun to feel genuinely baffled. To think that your woman is being cold to you because of another man is almost ennobling. Maybe he is throwing money at her. Maybe he is more good-looking than you. Women seem never able to resist shows . . . But to have to fight with your woman's career for her attention is not only new in the history of the world, but completely humiliating. In any case, how does one go about it? By the time Oko finally left Esi's place to take up his new post he was tired and bitter, and it all showed.

His people had of course learned of what had been going on between him and his wife. One day, one of his mothers and two of his sisters had marched on Esi, demanding what right she thought she had to start him on a new job with such bad luck? They had gone on to call her a semi-barren witch and told her that they thought their son and brother was well rid of her, thank God. Esi had not said a word during the entire performance.

In the end, even the practicalities of leaving a man who shared her accommodation had not proved too difficult for Esi to overcome. Especially since Oko had been only recently promoted – out of the classroom – to go and head a big secondary school in the mid-central region. She had made it clear to him that when he finally left Accra to go and assume duty in late August, she would not go with him then, and she would not join him later. Quite simple. Or that's what she had thought. Even then Oko had not really believed that Esi was serious, until she snubbed all his attempts to get her to see how his promotion would add some new advantages, and even glamour to their lives.

Esi had carried out her determination to leave Oko and even asked for a divorce. This development had so startled him that for a day or two he had almost become disorientated, and had taken to drinking a little more than usual. In fact, he was later aware that what had really saved him was the newest challenge in his life – going to head the school. It demanded so much of him he could not possibly have indulged in too much sorrowing after his collapsed marriage. But not even the new job could stop him from thinking about his broken marriage every now and then. He did, especially in the very late hours of the night, when he could finally leave his office and crawl home to bed. Sleeping alone did not feel right. After all, he hadn't done that for any consistent period for nearly ten years. But that was nothing compared to the real strangeness of not having the usual reminders of Esi around: the subtle aroma that was the sum total of her clothes, her perfumes, her powders, her body and even her briefcase and scribbling board. It was the absence of that and the sense of loss he suffered in consequence that so often assailed him mercilessly, and cruelly ruined his mornings. However, other aspects of his new job had in-built help for him. Since the school was some distance away from Accra, he was able to deceive himself into thinking that Esi had not left him. That they were only separated until she could start coming out for weekends. And he missed his daughter terribly too. Deep down in the corners of his being, he could not persuade himself to accept that it was all over.

Then Oko's mother came and deposited a breathing parcel on his doorstep, in the form of a very beautiful and very young girl. Oko was absolutely certain that he had not met her before. During their first encounter the only feeling he could recognise was extreme surprise – that it was still possible in this day and age to get a young woman in this world who would agree to be carried off as a wife to a man she had never met. He was also aware that he was too flattered to ask his mother to take her back. The young woman looked so soft and so easy, he found himself struggling not to think of her as too stupid to take Esi's place, even remotely. He soon found himself comparing the two women to beverages, and concluding that if Esi had been liquor this young woman was definitely going to be fruit juice. Being with Esi was being forever drunk. But he was also becoming convinced that she was not good for him. On the other hand, this specimen had brought with her a feeling of natural wholesomeness . . . So which ancestor first warned that turning down an offer of kingship does not necessarily mean that anyone is going to think of you when the matter of who to elect as the king's spokesman comes up? Oko let the girl stay.

When a letter arrived from a lawyer's office asking for a divorce for Esi, he was so mad he rushed to Accra. At first he threatened to refuse to divorce her. Then he changed his mind and talked reason. Sure, she could have a divorce if she could invent some grounds for it. He was not going to contest it. He was not even going to hire a lawyer to appear on his behalf in court. When Esi asked him about the girl, he just laughed and didn't even bother to ask how she knew. What he had asked her was not to be ridiculous. 'You know perfectly well that if ever you really want to, you can come back to me,' he said without the slightest trace of irony and cynicism, and left.

9

If Ali could not get Esi out of his system, it was not for
lack of trying. Growing up from boyhood into a man, he had
trained himself never to feel sexually attracted to other men's
women. It was part of what he had absorbed from his environment.
Spoken or unspoken, it was understood. No decent man did that
sort of thing. And if a man was not decent enough not to do it, then
he did not blame anybody if he got what came with such behaviour
– including death sometimes. He always remembered his father
telling or rather asking him in a discussion when he was only an
adolescent: 'But you see, my son, you know what my life is. How
do you think I could have survived all these years moving from
place to place, often sleeping in such odd conditions, if I had also
chased after other people's wives?' Ali could not have given an
answer even if one had been expected from him. Anyway, for him,
the whole issue had crystallised into a conviction that really there
was no need. Why go after other men's women when the world
had enough unattached females for each man to have his own and
some left over? And whether it was just an attitude or a
philosophy, it had worked until he met Esi.

After that first encounter in his office, Ali sat down and faced
the fact that Mrs Esi Sekyi excited him a great deal. But what
could he do about it? So there followed days when he would sit
behind his desk at Linga HideAways after office hours, pretending
he was working. In actual fact he was thinking about Esi. He had
started sending her presents. Then he had run into her by chance at
the Hotel Twentieth Century. After that, he gave up. He had to
seek her out, and he did.

After the great and endless agony he had gone through deciding whether or not he should contact her, what Ali had not at all been prepared for was to find Esi separated from her husband. As if that was not enough good news, one day he had learned, quite accidentally, that in fact she was divorced. From what she had told him as being the basis of her estrangement, he had thought she was crazy. Or rather, 'nicely mad'. Which was how he had put it to himself at the time. He had silently thanked Allah and set about wooing her.

The relationship between them soon became what could have been described as steady. If it had been in the village and within a strictly traditional setting, this was the point where some of her fathers would have marched on Ali to ask him what his intentions were. In the city, it only meant that Ali could take her out: to dinners and such. They always patronised restaurants that were hidden deep in the belly of the city, or far from the city centre along and the arteries that led motorists to other towns and even out of the country. These places had some things in common. They were dimly lit; they provided music for those who desired to dance anytime during the week, and couples could get keys . . .

However, Esi and Ali reserved their love-making for the comfort of Esi's bed. This nearly always followed an outing, as well as any time he came just to be with her. He would shut up Linga HideAways at the end of the working day and drive straight to her. They would immediately fall into each other's arms and hold her welcoming kiss from the front door through the length of the sitting-room, through her bedroom and on to her bed. Then for the next hour or so it was just grunts and groans until, quite exhaused, they fell quiet.

Since both of them would have had an exhausting day at their work places, they sometimes dozed off. Invariably, it was Ali who slept properly and longest. Esi would get up to go to the bathroom to wash herself and walk around for a while before looking for a cloth to wrap herself in. On days that she was absolutely certain she was not feeling up to a repeat of the love-making, she practically tiptoed around, careful not to wake Ali. For she knew what would happen if he woke up and saw her naked body.

Esi had always enjoyed walking around naked after love-making. For her, this was one of life's very few real luxuries.

Indeed, one miracle of her own existence was the fact that in spite of the torment she had suffered during childhood and adolescence for having an unfeminine body, as an adult she was not shy of showing that body to the men she slept with. As for walking around naked, she knew she could do that only when her fast growing child was out of the house, and the daily help had finished work and gone home. In fact, she had not gathered enough courage to sleep with Ali when either of those two or both of them were around. Already games were developing in the relationship, some of which were good, and others not so good. And one had to do with this business of Esi and nakedness . . .

Quite early in the relationship, Ali had sensed that Esi was struggling to feel easy about him watching her. So as if to encourage her boldness, he often pretended to be asleep so that he could lie there, aware of all the movements she made. It excited him enormously and was a source of one of the pleasures of being with her. He had slept with a great number of women in his time, but he knew very few women from his part of the world who even tried to be at ease with their own bodies. The combination of forces against that had been too overwhelming –

> traditional shyness and contempt for the biology of women;
> Islamic suppressive ideas about women;
> English Victorian prudery and French hypocrisy imported by the colonisers . . .

All these had variously and together wreaked havoc on the mind of the modern African woman: especially about herself. As far as Ali could tell, he told himself, most women behaved as if the world was full of awful things – beginning with their bodies. His wife Fusena, a good woman if ever there was one, was no exception. All the time they had lived practically alone in London, he never detected the faintest desire in Fusena ever to walk naked in the flat. And of course, with their present domestic set-up, there were always too many people around them for any body exhibitions anyway!

So being with Esi was altogether a change for Ali, for a number of other reasons too. For one, he was freed from the ordeal of having to find a place to be with a woman who was not his wife.

75

This was a problem which he knew some men faced. Especially those who liked younger women who had not become independent of their parents. The thought of sex with young girls made him shudder. Because, apart from the question of where to be with them, their inexperience filled him with a genuine feeling of horror. Being with Esi was also a rescue from the normal chaos of his existence. He could forget Linga for a while. He could also forget his home where, because of so many factors, privacy was a rare commodity. Here in this house, that was almost out of the city, he could unwind.

As he drifted into sleep after they had made love, Ali was thinking that it had been a good idea to send the deputy manager to the meeting in Las Palmas. He could see Esi every day for the next two weeks.

'Ali, Ali,' it was Esi's voice, coming to him from even further than the sitting room where she actually shouted from. His eyes flew open, and were immediately confronted by the vision of her in a wrap-around.

'Supper is ready,' she announced.

Food. Another source of pleasure when you were with Esi, Ali was thinking. She cooked like nobody else he knew or had known. In fact, until he met her, he had not considered fish as an edible protein. Now he wondered how in his previous existences he could have done without fried fish, stewed fish, grilled fish and especially softly smoked fish for so long. Fusena his wife was not at all a bad cook. But like him, she had come out of a meat-eating culture and dealing with fresh fish was not one of her stronger points in the kitchen.

Ali drew the cloth tightly round his body, even over his head, pretending as usual that he was asleep. Esi was forced to re-enter the bedroom.

'Ali, Ali,' Esi cried his name again, this time in a whisper. He nearly started to snore and the thought amused him so much, he himself began to laugh.

'Oh you,' exclaimed Esi, coming to sit by him. He tried to pull her down to him. She resisted firmly but unaggressively. He released her, and sat up.

'How do you know that food is what I want to eat right now?' he asked, taking hold of her and burying his head between her breasts.

'Food is what I want you to eat, this minute,' she replied, struggling somewhat for air.

'Okay, my lady's will shall be done,' he said, and he released her a second time. They both got up from the bed. 'But two things first,' he said running to the bathroom.

Esi went back to the kitchen, and was presently joined by Ali.

'So that was the first thing, which is the second thing?'

'A drink.'

Esi was repentant, apologetic and soothing. He was forgiving and soothing; assuring her that, after all, it was not really her fault. He hadn't given her much chance to offer him a drink, had he? And since they both knew what he was referring to, there was a short embarrassed space, until Esi asked him what he wanted to drink.

'What have you got?'

'Thanks to you, I've got just about everything, everything. Beer; wine: white, red, pink; rum: white and dark; proper scotch and all; vodka; cognac –'

He stopped her. He just wanted a beer.

'Are you sure?'

'Yes.'

She served him the beer and poured one for herself. Then they sat down to what had already become Ali's favourite meal at Esi's: grilled fish, usually sole or snapper on a platter with a slice of *kenkey* and a salad of fresh hot peppers, onions, tomatoes and salt. 'The usual', as any coastal man would have told him. Esi often protested that it was really a breakfast meal. Her protest fell on deaf ears. Of course, he appreciated anything she gave him. But this he could eat any hour, any day, every day. This evening it was sole, and, for the next hour, they ate in companionable silence from the same platter.

After the meal, Esi cleared the plates and went to dump them in the sink. As she was coming back to the table, she saw Ali emerging from the bedroom, dressed. She wondered aloud whether he was leaving, taking care not to let the mixture of her anxiety and disappointment show. But no, he said, not for some time, unless she wanted him to leave?

'No,' she replied simply.

'I just wanted to check on something in the car,' he offered, and went out.

The question of when Ali came to Esi's, and especially how long he stayed when he was there, had become another game which was already proving too dangerous to play. Ali was often out of Accra on business. And even when he was in town, he really could not see her every evening. Besides, he was also aware that when he came, there was what he himself considered to be a decent limit to how long he could stay. He loved Fusena his wife and tried not to hurt her deliberately. He knew she inevitably guessed when he was having a serious affair with another woman. Therefore the question was not whether he was deceiving her or not. There was an unspoken agreement between them not to talk about these affairs, that was all. But he always knew she knew. What he tried not to do was operate on the level of the kind of excesses which would leave her feelings unnecessarily bruised. In fact, he was not really capable of operating on that level. Or that was what he told himself. He was also too sensitive a father. He knew children would always have questions they would want to ask their parents. But then, neither the questions nor their answers need be too heavy for any young mind, he had told himself

Esi's grandmother could have told Ali that in the old days, there would have been no problem. 'Why marry two, three or more women if you were going to go through such contortions?' So no man who had more than one wife lived with any of the women on a permanent basis. Women could stay with their own people or you built each of them a small house if you were a man enough, because a woman had to have her own place. And the days were properly regulated. Wives took turns being wives. When it was one wife's turn, she cooked for the man and undertook the housekeeping for him completely. She either went to his bedroom or he slept with her. When her turn was over he just switched.

'And if a woman refused to leave when she had to?'

'Did you say when she had to?' She could not refuse. Everybody understood these things. There were no confusions.

'Supposing a man had a favourite?'

'He was not supposed to.'

'But that is a matter of the heart.'

'Ah, but that is why we do the serious business of living with our heads, and never our hearts.'

On her part, Esi at this stage was not really allowing herself to understand or not to understand Ali's comings and goings in relation to herself. She found the relationship very relaxing. She knew she had better leave well alone.

That had been a Thursday evening. When he was leaving, Ali had told Esi that he would be seeing her the next evening. She had not believed her ears. Two evenings in a row?

'It is surely going to rain,' she had murmured in his ear.

And it had rained . . . a somewhat unexpected downpour at that time of the year, when the rains were good. But then the rain had left a clear half of the total plantation of telephone poles on the ground.

Ali had not come that Friday evening as promised, or for the next two weeks. On Monday, Esi had tried to call his office but had not managed to get through. And it had taken all the strength she could muster not to go there in person . . . or try and phone his house.

In the course of building up whatever there now was between herself and Ali, Esi had laid down some rules for herself. One of the rules was that she would never never phone his house to ask for him. Another was not to make a habit of dropping into his office unexpectedly. These were clearly rules that were not going to be easy to obey. In fact, they often proved very difficult, and this was turning into one such time. The only solution to her restlessness was to keep busy. The days were no problem. The evenings were. Now she discovered the difference between not having people around but knowing where they are, and not having someone around and not knowing where he or she is. She also missed her daughter. For the first time, she was completely alone; and that made a big bag of emptiness to handle. *Nyenyefo mpo wo ne nkaeda* – having to love a burdensome child because one day you will miss her. Trust our elders to come out with a proverb to describe every situation.

Suddenly, the tropical nights had become dark, hot and heavy with all manner of threats.

10

The next time Ali showed up at Esi's was late morning on a Sunday. It had rained the night before, as it had done most nights of the previous week. Sometimes it had rained in the day too, and occasionally non-stop for a solid twenty-four-hour period. The sea was brimming and green. The grasses and leaves of the giant *nim* trees stood or hung at their greenest and silvery with raindrops. The world was slaked, content and quiet.

Esi had woken up feeling fine. The previous evening, she had gone to Oko's mother to see Ogyaanowa. There had been some tensions as soon as she entered the house. Leaving them she had told herself that if she could only stop herself from missing the child so much, she would just stop going to that place. But she couldn't. One Saturday, she had decided not to go. As some test of her willpower. It had not worked. That weekend, she had experienced a strange restlessness. The following weekdays the restlessness had become so intense she had finally relaxed only after she had gone to see the child on Wednesday evening after work.

This morning she had stayed late in bed reading. When she finally got up, it was to have a shower and get into a pair of shorts and a much-worn loose shirt that was something of a favourite. Next, she had rummaged through her rather impressive music library for some choral music. She smiled to herself as she remembered what her grandmother had said about that the last time she had been around for one of her very short visits. When Esi put on the cassette tape with her special selection of local Christian music, Nana had pointedly put one ear near the recorder. She had nodded her head and hummed along with the group who were singing: obviously enjoying herself.

Then when it was all over, she had looked straight at Esi: 'My lady, if you want to be with your God on a Sunday morning, just get yourself to church.'

At that, Esi had protested that we can worship God everywhere and at any time.

'Why did our ancestors build the shrines and the white people build their churches then?'

The two of them had had one of their long and friendly arguments. Obviously, the older woman had read her. As usual. This time to discover that because she was too lazy to go to church, she played Christian music on Sunday mornings so that she would not feel too guilty.

Now to guilt was added shame. But the hardest habits to break are our lazy ones. So here she was again, turning over her albums and her tapes. Later, the issue of what to play settled, she had sat down to her standard Sunday morning breakfast of *dokon-na-kyenam*. She was just thinking that after all living alone was not the unpleasant business people made it seem, when she heard the sound of a car pull up at the gate.

She drew a curtain to see who it was. It was Ali. She went outside to open the gate. He drove into the courtyard. She locked the gate again, and strolled after the car.

Esi was truly delighted to see Ali who in the meantime had brought his car to a standstill behind hers. She put her head through the window on the passenger side of the front seats and said, 'Hello.'

'Hello, Esi,' replied Ali, equally delighted. He jumped out of the car, and they both entered the house. As soon as Esi had shut the front door behind them, they embraced. Following their usual practice, Ali was clearly embarking on a long kiss which would have ended on Esi's bed. But although she had missed him rather badly, or rather, because she had, and was somewhat afraid of what it would all mean in the long run, she was not going to have any of that. At least, not yet. Ali immediately sensed her reluctance, and withdrawing a little from her, asked her 'why' with his eyes.

'Don't you think we should do some talking first?'

'No, I don't think so. Talking can be done anytime.'

'Not always, Ali,' she said uncertainly. 'Sometimes things get too late even for talk.'

'Okay. I believe I owe you some explanation for promising to come the other day, and then not showing up for two weeks.'

Relief flooded through her. She was grateful that he had recognised that something had not been correct.

'Yes,' she said, eagerly.

'But don't you think I could have a proper welcome first?' Ali was persistent. Esi wasn't yielding either. By this time, they were standing in the middle of the sitting room. 'But can I at least sit down?' Ali asked.

'Yes, of course,' said Esi, with a voice that clearly said that even that was a big decision to make. Ali sat on the couch and patted the space by him for Esi to sit down. She did.

'Actually, I tried to phone.'

'Then you might as well have saved your energies,' she said with something like resignation. 'We all know the phones –'

'They hardly work at the best of times. And with the recent merciful downpour, and possibly all the poles down, they'll stay dead until the end of the century!'

'Oh Africa. Fancy a normal blessing like rain coming to us with strings,' Esi said with a very big sigh.

Ali protested vigorously at her tone and reminded her that after all, Allah had been kind to the continent and its people. What was causing some confusions was inefficiency.

'Drought and all?' Esi wondered, uncertainly.

'Drought and all.' Ali had no such doubts. As far as he could see, given the enormous resources of the continent, even solving the problems that natural disasters such as drought created should not have been difficult if people worked seriously. Spoken with such earnestness, Esi had to see his point. So they both laughed a little bitterly and scolded themselves for being too serious and consequently depressing themselves on a beautiful morning. After that, Ali rushed through his explanations for that long period of absence. How it had occurred to him that it was vitally important that he checked his telex machine. And so from her place he had driven back to his office instead of going home, and on and on and on. Esi accepted all that. What else could she do? She knew that Ali knew that she had to believe any movements he claimed he had had to make based on messages received on the telex machine. Although of course there always were other factors. She could only guess at these because she did not know enough about his life to make any other type of deductions. And what use is guess work most of the time?

Ali had had the telex machine installed in his office when it became clear that the agency's business was expanding sufficiently to make the acquisition of such a facility worthwhile. Fairly soon after that, it occurred to him that messages come in at odd hours because people have a tendency not only to finalise travel and holiday plans at odd hours but also immediately to move to do something about them. Besides, there was also the matter of time differences between the countries of the world. He had therefore told himself that since he was not the head of a government department, and since he could not pretend to afford to run a nine-to-five schedule, the least he could do was, once an evening, to go and check on the telex machine. Although it was already possible for him to delegate such duties even by the time he met Esi, and in the meantime he had disciplined himself to see that, except matters of life and death, nearly every issue can wait to be handled in the light of the next day, he kept up the practice of occasionally checking on the telex.

There had been one other reason why Ali went to his office first after leaving Esi's instead of going straight home. It was not something he could tell Esi. In fact, he couldn't have told anyone else but himself – that it was an essential part of managing his situation.

Again, by the time Esi became part of his life, Ali had learnt to expect Fusena to phone his office if he was not at home by a certain time in the evening. He had never believed in making a bedroom of his office. He knew that some executives did. But he was aware that Fusena had her own ideas about what he stayed up there so late to do so often. So although he had given up trying to dispel her suspicions, he had decided that at least it helped if he was sometimes in when she rang. In fact, one evening Fusena had been so suspicious that she had actually driven over to check things up for herself. Ali had been absolutely alone. Fusena had felt so ashamed, she had never repeated the trip. But once in a while, when the waiting got really unbearable, she still rang and he always enjoyed taking those late night calls. There are few pleasures left, and surely one of them must be having the chance to prove you are a faithful spouse – especially when you are not.

So from Esi's place, he continued. He had passed through his office, and sure enough a couple of messages had come through after they had closed for the day. In fact, one of them was from Abidjan, and it sounded as if a major crisis were brewing in the office there. It was clear he would have to get there the following morning, although he did not like the idea. After all, hadn't he just made some other adjustments to enable him to stay put for a while for among other reasons, to be with Esi? Anyway, he had stayed in the office to put some papers together. Then it had started to rain. He had rushed home. As Esi also knew, it had rained all that night. The next morning he had passed through his office on his way to the airport and tried to phone her from there.

'And the rest, as they say, is history!' Esi finished for him.

'Thank you,' said Ali, giving her a squeeze on the ribs. As he was speaking, Ali himself was aware that he had to make sure that that sort of thing did not happen again. He made a silent vow to put some machinery into motion to take care of such emergencies. But one should be careful not to make too many promises too early, he also silently warned himself.

'But you could have asked one of your people from the office to bring me a message.' It was as if she had read his mind.

'Yes, Esi, and I'm ashamed of myself for not thinking about it.' The confession was made with great charm and accompanied by another squeezing of her ribs.

'Can you forgive me?' he pleaded.

'Well . . .' Esi began playfully. Ali stopped whatever she might have had in mind to say. He started to kiss her rather hungrily, and proceeded to undress her at the same time.

'Let's at least go to the bedroom . . .'

'No . . .'

Then starting from the top of her head, he began to feel her all over, with his eyes tightly shut, and therefore genuinely groping like a blind person. Each time he touched any part of her that he found specially erotic, a massive shudder shook him. It happened with her nose, her mouth, her breast. By the time he got to her pubic hairs, he could not hold himself any longer. He moved to part Esi's legs. But the legs parted for him, willingly. And then he was inside her, feeling his way into a cave that was warm, of uneven surfaces, wet and dangerously inviting . . . On her part Esi felt somewhat cramped because the couch was rather narrow. But then she also thought that she would rather not be comfortable if it would mean having to give up all those different kinds and levels of sensations she was enjoying without shame. She wanted to scream, and scream and scream.

It is not possible to feel like this on this earth, she was thinking. And nothing is as sweet as being inside a woman, he was thinking. Then both of them were moaning and moaning and moaning.

Some weeks later, Ali went to Esi's clearly in a pensive mood. She noticed it immediately. They drank, made love, listened to music. Ali wasn't talking much. And Esi had never believed in forcing conversation on people anyway. She let him be.

When Ali finally spoke aloud, Esi was a little startled.

'You know Esi, I keep wondering . . .'

'What about?'

'I keep wondering how any one woman can be as beautiful as you are, and still manage to be so clever.'

Esi laughed aloud with sheer relief. She had feared that when he opened his mouth it would be about something very serious.

'Please Ali, don't flatter.'

'It is the truth.'

'Okay, I too keep wondering how any one man can be so handsome as you look and still manage to be so sharp.'

'We are not talking about me,' Ali said authoritatively.

'Yes we are . . . And by the way, you haven't told me when you came back from your last trip!'

'Just last night.'

'Ei, really?' Esi's surprise showed.

'But did you think that I could be back in this city for over twenty-four hours without trying to see you?'

'Oh well,' said Esi, shrugging her shoulders shyly. 'I missed you too.'

'Did you? True, true?' Ali was delighted.

'True, true. And in any case, why do you sound so surprised?'

'Well . . . it's just that you don't strike me as someone who'll miss anybody.'

This time the surprise was not so pleasant. In fact, she almost felt rebuked.

'How do I strike you?'

'Just kind of relaxed . . . like . . . like . . . as if you don't need anybody.'

Ali was groping somewhat because he realised that even if he knew what he wanted to say, he was not sure any more that that was the way he had wanted to say it.

'Thank God that outward looks can be so deceptive. Ali, there isn't a single human being who doesn't need somebody.'

'Does that mean you will marry me?'

'Must I?'

'Yes Esi, I want to marry you.'

Esi suffered a jolt. Right from the beginning of their affair, Ali had been dropping these hints which she had simply refused to take seriously. Now put so bluntly, there was no way she could pretend she had not heard him. However, she knew that by marriage he also meant her becoming his second wife. Although the idea fascinated her no end, she could sense that it meant complications.

'And your wife?' It was Ali's turn to be startled. It had not occurred to him that asking such a question was what her first reaction to his proposal would be. 'Where does she come in?' Esi could only laugh like an indulgent parent. 'Everywhere . . . What does she feel about it? Or you have not discussed your plans for me with her?'

'I have,' said Ali, too quickly, too loudly.

He was clearly nervous, since he knew that he was not speaking the truth. He tried to convince Esi not to worry about the feelings of Fusena. He had discussed everything with her, he insisted, and that Fusena had even expressed gratitude for having been warned, since it would save her the shame of being the public's laughing stock. That is, if everyone knew what was going on and she didn't, and on and on and on. But Esi was not at all fooled. Ali was a man who exuded assurance every minute of the day. And therefore to see him betray the slightest bit of nervousness was somewhat pathetic. The result was that for some time that Sunday afternoon, there were too many uncomfortable gaps in their conversation.

After a while Ali managed to switch the discussion to whether Esi had managed to talk to her mother about them. It was now her turn to be nervous.

'Yes,' she said too quietly, too slowly.

'And what was her reaction? . . . What did she she say?'

According to Esi, her mother had said a lot. A whole lot, in fact. What she did not tell Ali was that her grandmother had said even more.

'She doesn't like me?' Ali wondered.

'Oh, she likes you all right,' she said light-heartedly. 'Which daughter's mother wouldn't? All those presents you unload on her doorstep?'

'But Esi, presents or no presents, your mother may not want to see my face!' he exclaimed.

Esi couldn't believe her ears. How had he come by such insight? She was too honest to argue with him over that particular fact. Therefore she made the issue somewhat general. She said that she was not sure her mother did not like him. It was not him. It was the question of her being a second wife. Her mother did not like that. Her mother thought it was a sort of come down for her. Ali listened carefully to her and then asked her a rather strange question.

'Esi, did your mother like your ex-husband?'

By now she was thinking that the afternoon or Ali was bringing out too many surprises.

'Frankly, yes. Very much.' She told the truth. Her mother liked Oko. In fact her mother had sometimes behaved as if Oko was her son and she the daughter-in-law, when it came to matters to do with their marriage. She couldn't have made Ali angrier if she had calculated.

'I'm very sure she is not going to like me at all . . . It is obvious, it is impossible.'

'But Oko is that kind of a man.'

'What kind of a man?' Ali was feeling jealous and not even trying to hide it.

'You know, the kind of man who brings out all of a woman's mothering instincts up front.' In her anxiety to soothe, she tried to say more. But it turned out that everything she said was also the worst thing to say. It was that kind of occasion. 'Even Opokuya liked him,' she said.

'Is that your friend? The one I met at the Hotel Twentieth Century?'

'Yes.'

'You appeared to be quite intimate . . . and so she likes your ex-husband very much. Do you also like her husband?' He was feeling quite grouchy.

'Don't be nasty, Ali,' said Esi. She was feeling rather sad about the way things had gone. 'We've been friends for a very long time . . . since we were in school. In fact, we are really like sisters.'

'Does that mean she should like your husband?'

'Well . . . yes. She . . . I mean, she sort of approved of him.' But she had regretted introducing the whole idea into the discussion. Except that there was nothing she could do about it at that stage. As for Ali, he was feeling very frustrated.

'I see . . . I can see what I'm up against,' he said, 'because I don't think I arouse any woman's mothering instincts.'

Esi jumped at the opportunity.

'Oh, my dear,' she began, full of sweet comfort. 'Don't you see that's why I like you so much? After all, if I'd wanted to mother someone's grown-up son, I would have stayed with Oko.'

Ali was only mildly pacified. 'So what am I supposed to do?'

There was another of those disturbing pauses. Then he said, with some vehemence, 'Esi, I just want you to be my wife. Very much. That's all.'

All Esi could do was to assure him that perhaps the situation with her mother wasn't completely hopeless. She suspected that although her mother may not approve of her being someone's second wife, she may prefer that to nothing . . . of Esi just having an affair with him and staying forever as his mistress. Since Ali was quite anxious about the whole situation, he then proposed that they go to see her fathers. Esi thought that was fine. Ali wanted to go and see them the next day. Esi thought that would be ridiculously early. She thought she needed to do some basic organisation first. Besides, her people didn't consider Saturdays as good days for betrothals and such. Ali of course wanted to know why not.

'Something to do with Saturday being a masculine day. You see, to our people, the days of the week are divided into those that are feminine and the rest which are masculine. Sundays, Tuesdays, Thurs –'

But Ali was impatient. Eventually they agreed on a Sunday about a month ahead, depending of course on whether or not Esi's fathers wanted to see Ali at all. When he started rummaging through the pockets of his rather voluminous *agbada*, Esi wondered what he was looking for. He soon pulled out a small box, flipped it open and revealed a gold ring worked over with fine filigree for which that area was so well known.

Esi couldn't believe her eyes, and she soon couldn't believe her ears either.

'Bring your finger,' Ali commanded.

'Ali!' she could only exclaim.

'Come on, come on, bring it.'

Esi brought out her finger rather gingerly. It was almost as if she was afraid of the ring. But Ali seized it and slipped the ring on it.

'Oh Ali, it is beautiful,' she said in a breathless whisper.

'Do you really think so?'

'Of course.'

'Wear it for me then.'

'But why?'

'What do you mean by "but why?" I thought you had agreed to be my wife.'

'Are you saying that this is some kind of an engagement ring?'

'Definitely.'

'But Ali –'

'What?'

'I thought I was only going to be your second wife.'

'What difference should that make? And what is this about "only a second wife"? Isn't a wife a wife?'

'Okay. Okay. What I mean is that you have already got Fusena who was your first wife. She wears your ring, and I'm almost certain that here in this city she is the only one known as Mrs Kondey.'

'Yes, but only officially or formally. Most people, our friends and neighbours call her Adam-Maami, after our older son . . .'

'Ali, you know what I'm trying to say . . .'

'Maybe. But Esi, what has all that got to do with you wearing my ring?'

'Ali, Fusena already wears your ring.'

'What you mean is that she wears one of my rings.'

Esi just sat: stunned with the wonder and the puzzle of it all.

In a short while, she recovered enough to ask Ali whether what they were doing was not bigamy. Ali exploded.

'When put like that, yes, we are committing a crime. Polygamy, bigamy. To the people who created the concepts, these are all crimes. Like homicide, rape and arson. Why have we got so used to describing our cultural dynamics with the condemnatory tone of our masters' voices? We have got marriage in Africa, Esi. In Muslim Africa. In non-Muslim Africa. And in our marriages a man has a choice – to have one or more wives.' He paused dramatically, and then ended with a flourish: 'As long as he can look after them properly.'

Esi had never seen the whole Islamic thing about marriage in such terms. Ever. And she knew that what he was saying was absolutely right. She couldn't help feeling somewhat ashamed. At the same time, what she couldn't sort out was the very loyally indigenous viewpoint and the fact that his ring was shining on her finger at that material time.

'Ali, I'm sorry. But the ring, this ring, it's not exactly a part of our way of doing the two or more wives business, is it?'

'No, I mean not according to recent traditions. But let's look at it carefully. Besides, as usual, it probably started with our ancient Egyptian ancestors. In fact, we hear they did. Lovers exchanging rings and all that. In any case, the business of asking a betrothed to begin wearing a ring is a damned useful custom, whoever started it. And a betrothed is a betrothed whether she is the first betrothed or fourth betrothed. You've agreed to be my wife, Esi, you start wearing my ring.'

'But why should it be so necessary?' Esi was not getting any clearer about the ring, and she decided it would be better if she didn't pretend to be.

'Why Esi, for the same reason that any betrothed or married woman would wear any man's ring. To let the rest of the male world know that she is bespoke.'

'That she has become occupied territory?'

'Yes, that she has become occupied territory.'

Esi was thinking that the whole thing sounded so absolutely lunatic and so 'contemporary African' that she would save her sanity probably by not trying to understand it. The only choice left to her was to try and enter into the spirit of it. So she suggested to Ali that if that was the case, then he should take the ring back, and give it to her with her people looking on, after they had gone to them and all the negotiations were completed.

'No,' Ali was short and clear, 'this you wear from today. What I give you before your people will be a marriage ring.'

At that, Esi just threw back her head and laughed and laughed – at the insolence of the modern African male. Tears were streaming down her face.

'Why, what's so funny?' Ali seemed genuinely mystified.

'Oh . . . Ali . . . Oh . . . Ali . . . Ali . . .' Esi tried several times to explain what she found so highly amusing. She failed each time; she was stammering, stuttering and positively gasping for air.

After some time, she grew calm and Ali said he wanted a beer and went to fetch himself one. When he asked Esi if she wanted a drink, she just said not really, maybe she would take a sip from his glass. But Ali brought her a separate glass anyway. And it was soon clear why. When he put his glass to his lips, he gulped its contents down in huge mouthfuls. When he finished, he groaned appreciatively, 'Eh God . . . I needed that.'

'You sound as if you've just come through a battle.'

'Wasn't there one?' he asked, pretending genuine curiosity. He took another swig of beer.

They spent the rest of the afternoon planning the trip to go see her people. They went over and over the required items. They also agreed that since custom did not permit them to drive down in the same vehicle, they would have to travel separately and if possible, she a day earlier. He would have to go with somebody, a man, a close friend or relative, since no man was expected to enter into such negotiations alone.

As the red of sunset broke through the *nim* trees, Ali pronounced that he would have to go home. Esi didn't think it was necessary to protest. It had been a full day, to say the least.

11

From the day he put his ring on her finger, Ali became a more frequent visitor at Esi's. It was not strange then that one day, just as his car was going out of her gate, Opokuya's was about to pull into the drive from the main road, wanting to get in. He stopped, backed and pulled aside. Esi opened the gate again and Opokuya drove in. Ali jumped out of his car, waved to stop a bemused Opokuya, greeted her, jumped back into his car and was gone.

Opokuya could hardly contain herself long enough to park her car properly. She removed her foot so hastily from the accelerator that the poor engine spluttered to a stop, jerking the car so much that she herself was thrown against the steering wheel. When she got out of her car, she immediately launched into her apologies and explanations of why she had not been able to see Esi in such a long time.

On her part, Esi was just happy to see her and was therefore forgiving. In any case, she was not in a position to complain, she offered. Since she had broken up with Oko she had become so nervous at the prospect of a meeting and a possible confrontation between her and Kubi that she had virtually stopped going to Sweet Breezes Hill. Opokuya understood. But then it also meant that they met only when Opokuya drove over – which could not be very often, considering her packed life, and the everlasting *wahala* with Kubi over the car.

Opokuya noticed the ring on Esi's finger. Not that she was doing anything to hide it. Opokuya was curious. Esi didn't disappoint her. Upon hearing all about it, Opokuya remarked that if she were a white woman, she would have fainted away. But as an African woman, she could only do her thing, which was exclaiming 'Ei, ei' several times over, marching up and down the length of the sitting room, and finally taking hold of Esi's hand, having a proper look at it and asking whether she was sure of what she was saying. Meanwhile, Esi kept on laughing with delight. After they had both exhausted themselves, they sat down to have a drink and some serious chat.

Opokuya said something to the effect that obviously she needn't ask Esi how she was. She had noticed that both she and Ali looked superb. Esi purred and showed Opokuya the various presents Ali had brought her from his travels: an elegant piece of Makonde sculpture; several huge bottles of her favourite perfume; a dyed damask shawl; a pair of outrageously big and gorgeous Sub-Sahelian gold earrings which she definitely didn't have adequate holes in her ears ever to wear . . . There was even a fancy digital clock-radio, which was at the time perhaps one of the very first to arrive at the Guinea coast from some plant in South-East Asia where such toys were being churned out for the junk-consuming markets of Africa.

'You lucky, lucky girl.' Opokuya was honestly envious.

'I must confess that at this moment I feel very much like an empress receiving tribute from an over-anxious warlord,' Esi agreed with Opokuya with wicked delight.

'Well enjoy them, Your Imperial Majesty. And here's to a happy marriage.' Opokuya raised her glass.

'Opokuya, you don't sound convinced.'

'Are you convinced?'

'Yes, I am.'

'Then I should be. Because what is important is what you feel.'

'Opokuya, Ali is wonderful. And so understanding of the kind of woman I am.'

Opokuya's eyelids raised themselves up a fraction.

'Handsome too. And so obviously generous.'

'Too, too generous.' It was almost becoming a contest of who praised Ali most. And Esi thought she definitely ought to out-do Opokuya in that. 'And so mature,' she added.

'The way things are going, I could quite easily swop my dear Kubi,' Opokuya said seriously.

'Now I know you are teasing . . . but by the way, my sister, after we've gone to see my people and everything has been sorted out, I'll want to throw a small party. You and Kubi must come. Please?'

'I don't know about that . . . Oh, I will come. But I'm not sure about Kubi.' Opokuya was feeling uncomfortable. And that immediately sobered Esi. She tried to change the subject by asking about Opokuya's children. Then inevitably Opokuya asked about Oko. No, Esi hadn't heard of him for months. No, they were not really in touch. She had bumped into him once or twice when she had gone to visit Ogyaanowa at his mother's. But they didn't behave like two long-lost friends. Yes, the divorce was quite final.

Then she quickly moved back to the plans she and Ali had made about going to see her people. Could Opokuya come with her? They were both aware that under normal circumstances this would have been proper and nice. But Opokuya, who did not feel too good about the whole business, was able to turn down the invitation with a genuine excuse. She had to be at work on that particular Sunday because some women's charity group had promised to come and visit the hospital with what sounded like a large consignment of blankets, bandages, sheeting and other items they needed rather badly.

For a while, neither of them spoke. Then Esi said, her voice a mixture of a complaint and an appeal. 'Opokuya, you still think I should have stayed married to Oko?'

'And your mother, what does she think?'

Esi tried not to resent the very obvious evasion.

'To be honest, she doesn't like the divorce . . . and she hates the idea of me becoming anyone's second wife.'

'Hmm. That's serious. I would have thought a woman like your mother who still lives in the village would have understood.'

'That's what I had also thought. But quite clearly we were all wrong. My mother thinks that with all the education I've had, I should have everything better than she has had.'

'Including a monogamous marriage?'

'Sort of . . . In actual fact, I don't think she sees it in terms of monogamous and polygamous marriages.'

'Y-e-s?'

'You see, with her, it's a question of me having my own husband.'

'Like Oko?'

'Yes, like Oko. She thinks I deserve better than having to share someone's man. Or having to go into someone's marriage, as she would rather put it.'

'I see. Does that mean that she wouldn't have minded if it was your husband who had brought another woman into your marriage?'

'Yes. I mean, no. To her, that would not have been a problem to worry about. Not at all. Because you see then I would be the senior wife. In traditional terms, still "the wife". And in today's terms too. And she reminds me of this all the time. I would be the one to whom the title of "Mrs" legitimately belonged. I would be the "Mrs".'

'The seniority too. Esi, it seems perfectly reasonable for a mother to see the distinction in the two positions and have a preference on behalf of her daughter.'

'Opoku, you are so right. And you are not only right; in fact, if I know my mother, she would have lectured me on how to make the other woman feel at home, if Oko had brought some woman into our marriage!'

For some time, the two women were quiet.

Suddenly, Opokuya got up and rushed out. She soon returned with the most beautiful woven tray Esi had ever seen. It was perfectly oval, with two sturdy handles and a base that glimmered like a golden rainbow.

'Actually I've kept it for you for over a year, if you can believe that,' she was panting as she was offering it to Esi. 'I bought it when I was home last year. But you know me, I've always forgotten to give it to you. I suspect I've even brought it as far as here, not once, twice or . . .'

Esi hadn't heard a word. 'Opokuya, just thank you, thank you. But you could have waited a little longer and given it to me for my Christmas present or birthday or something.'

'Don't be funny Esi. You know we are not in the habit of exchanging gifts on occasions like birthdays. Considering I never even remember my own birthday. As for Christmas . . . we'll celebrate it when it comes.'

There was another long pause during which Esi kept turning the tray round and round, admiring the patterns.

'But my objections are different,' said Opokuya. Esi didn't show any surprise. It was not necessary for her to ask Opokuya what she was referring to. She knew.

'What are they?'

'Esi, if we go on with this talk, I suspect I shall begin to sound as if I want to pour cold water on your happiness.'

'Go on.'

'Well, it's just that I feel . . . I feel . . . Look here, Esi, for example, can you see yourself and Ali's wife getting together? . . . Being friends? . . . You know, for instance getting together about Ali's strengths and occasionally trading gossip about his weaknesses? Can you see that happening?'

The idea seemed so unlikely that Esi couldn't believe she was hearing right. Be friends with Ali's wife? Trade gossip with Ali's wife?

'I don't even know what she looks like,' she blurted out.

'You see,' said Opokuya, with something like a minor triumph, 'first rule already broken.'

'Really?' Esi asked with genuine curiosity.

'Of course, Esi. In the village, or rather in a traditional situation, it was not possible for a man to consider taking a second wife without the first wife's consent. In fact, it was the wife who gave the new woman a thorough check-over right at the beginning of the affair. And her stamp of approval was a definite requirement if anything was to become of the new relationship.'

'Oh really?' said Esi again.

'So where did you grow up?' Opokuya realised she didn't know her friend as much as she had thought she did. Esi's level of naïvety clearly bordered on the dangerous. How could she . . .?

'I'll ask Ali to let his wife meet me before we go to see my people,' Esi said a little defiantly, a little fearfully.

'Fine.'

Esi asked Opokuya whether she should fix them something to eat. But Opokuya declined. She had to be moving.

A certain knot of anxiety which seemed to have built in Esi refused to go away. She said, in an attempt to reassure herself, 'Listen, Opokuya, you often accuse me of lacking passion. But I think I care very much for Ali. And we are going to try and be very happy, he and I. Please try to understand.'

'But sure,' said Opokuya, 'I understand. I think you are brave for wanting to try –'

'An alternative lifestyle?' asked Esi, rather wickedly.

'Yes, an alternative lifestyle.' Then at once they were both relaxed again. They were sisters and both knew it felt good.

Opokuya got up, gathered her handbag and began to look for her keys.

'You don't want another drink?'

Opokuya shook her head.

'Not one small one for the road?'

Opokuya shook her head, rather vigorously, and playfully. She turned to Esi once she had found her car keys, which she was twirling around.

'My dear, don't look so sad. You'll be all right.' What she wanted to add but which she didn't, was that it was meaningless for Esi to say that she and Ali were going to be happy. In a polygamous situation, or rather in the traditional environment in which polygamous marriages flourished, happiness, like most of the good things of this life, was not a two-person enterprise. It was the business of all parties concerned. And in this case it should have included the first wife of Ali whom Esi had not even met!

'Opokuya, monogamy is so stifling.' Esi said this almost desperately and uncannily, as though she was answering Opokuya's thoughts.

'I suspect you mean marriage,' Opokuya shot back in parting.

They were both laughing again as Esi took Opokuya to her car.

12

Some people are born in this world who show by their actions throughout their lives that they come from the 'never-give-up' section of the spirit world. Ali was one of them. He had decided to marry Esi. And so marry her he was going to.

The first time Ali informed Fusena that he was thinking of taking a second wife, Fusena asked him, before the words were properly out of his mouth, 'She has a university degree?'

This was nowhere near what Ali had expected from her in the way of response. So he too asked, 'What has that got to do with it?'

'Everything,' she shot back. She picked up her handbag and her basket, left the bedroom, came out to the courtyard, issued instructions in very quick successions to her household – and whoever might have been around – on food, what to do that day about fetching the children from school and from the day nursery, and on and on, and then she left the house. Before starting her car, which was a small two-door vehicle she had come to love unreasonably and fiercely, she removed her veil completely and put it together with the handbag on the passenger seat next to her. The car screeched into life, and Fusena backed out so roughly, she nearly scraped one side of her husband's rather elegant and capacious chariot, and also nearly hit the family dog. She was on her way out for the day to manage the kiosk.

Fusena's movements were most clearly out of gear that morning. Normally, Ali left the house first. Although the Achimota/Nima/Barracks intersection where the kiosk stood was not far from the house, she had not made it a habit of regularly popping home from the shop to check on her duties as a housewife. She took all her jobs seriously. When she was in the kiosk, she was there. And of course when she was home, she was home. That was why she took so much time in the morning leaving the house. She took time organising herself and the house. It was something she enjoyed. She checked on her wardrobe, her hair and even her nails. She planned the meals for the household for the day and virtually planned the rest of their housekeeping for months ahead. She was one of the wives in the country who could still do that. And that was only because she was married to a man who cared about how his home ran. And since his job demanded a lot of travelling he always made it a point of getting things that were necessary for his home – depending of course on where he went. For most other women it had become a question of buying what you found in the shops or the markets when you found them. Efficient housekeeping in such circumstances had nothing to do with planning. Every other wife in their circle of friends envied Fusena. Yet here she was feeling so sorry for herself, she could quite literally die. She had allowed Ali to talk her out of teaching, hadn't she? And now the monster she had secretly feared since London had arrived. Her husband had brought into their marriage a woman who had more education than she did.

The streak of abnormality managed to run through some more of that morning. When Fusena drove to the kiosk the first time, she did not go in. After she had parked and was getting out of the car, she changed her mind, banged shut the car door which she had just opened and drove back to the house. She met Ali in front of their gate just as he was backing out. She drove her car to where the two cars became parallel, and stopped. Ali had stopped, and looked at her with a question on his face.

'Is she also a Muslim?' Fusena asked him, without any prelims, and without getting out.

Caught unawares for the second time that early morning, Ali said just simply, 'No.' Fusena backed out again and drove off. She was going to look for someone to talk to.

Part II

Said Aba to Ama:

      My sister, the number of reasons for which men leave their women for other women –

Ama: Or just add those new women to their older ones . . .

Aba: – are many.

Ama: And becoming more and more.

Aba: It used to be beauty.

Ama: And being younger.

Aba: More energy to work the fields, strong legs and better hips to make babies with. It is still beauty and being younger. But now there is also –

Ama: There was always a woman's birth. We should not forget that.

Aba: You mean family wealth and influence?

Ama: Yes. Who the father was. And the mother too.

Aba: Cabinet ministers are high on the list.

Ama: Let us say people in government.

Aba: But then let us just say people with power: kings and queens and those who are near kings and queens.

Ama: Chiefs and warlords, powerful priests and controllers of purses . . .

Aba: Leaders of secret societies.

Ama: Prime ministers, presidents, general secretaries of free republics, secretary generals –

Aba: And those who are near prime ministers, presidents, general secretaries of free republics, secretary generals.

Ama: Heads of corporations, especially transnationals.

101

Aba:	Big time professionals and top international civil servants.
Ama:	UN this and UN that.
Aba:	UNDP, UNESCO and other UN organs.
Ama:	Regional bodies.
Aba:	Sub-regional bodies.
Ama:	Doctors.
Aba:	Engineers.
Ama:	Judges and lawyers.
Aba:	So then, publishers! We could say very simply that it was –
Ama:	And is!
Aba:	– sometimes, the daughters of the people with power.
Ama:	People who make the wheel of life turn.
Aba:	And what such people owned in lands and houses . . .
Ama:	Jewels and cash.
Aba:	Cattle, sheep and goats.
Ama:	Kola pits.
Aba:	Cocoa farms.
Ama:	Coffee plantations.
Aba:	Import and export businesses.
Ama:	Now it's also cars that race for money, horses with jockeys, aeroplanes.
Aba:	We must not forget that these days it could be the woman herself who would have such power.
Ama:	Indeed it is not necessary for her to be anybody's daughter if she has the power of beauty, of youth, political, financial . . .
Aba:	A top athlete, a film star!
Ama:	Nor should we forget high education, a degree or two.
Aba:	A government job with side benefits.
Ama:	One of the topmost posts.
Aba:	One of the largest pay packets!

13

One Sunday in the month of July, which was also the Republic Day holiday weekend, Ali took the deputy manager of Linga HideAways with him and drove to Esi's village. They were going to see her people. When they got there, Ali discovered that he had brought trouble to Palaver Town. Esi's fathers proceeded to grill him mercilessly. To some questions they found his answers quite satisfactory: to others not at all. Two points engaged their attention more than any others, and it became clear fairly early in the discussions that on account of one of them or both, they would send him packing back to Accra. One was on whether his wife knew of his intentions in connection with Esi, and the other was this business of having no-one in the whole wide world to take along there except someone from his own firm.

'How much can any man's employees know about him?' someone asked.

'And even more important, you don't just take anybody to be a witness at your marriage negotiation!' a second added.

'No,' a third answered him. 'You take someone who by age, kinship, social standing or wealth is in a position to stand firm in all matters to do with the well-being of that marriage. Above all, he or she must be one who in a crisis must be respected and deferred to by all parties concerned. Your own employee? No-no.'

In the end, it became clear that as far as they were concerned, it all boiled down to who was backing the marriage from Ali's side. To which Ali had confessed that he could not produce anybody. All his people were up north.

'So exactly to whom are we supposed to give our daughter in marriage?' Esi's fathers wanted to know. After all, in the world they knew, a marriage involved the two families. Each group thoroughly vetted the other, to the extent that sometimes either or both sides employed the services of paid spies who went through everything with a fine-toothed comb: people's histories, their social reputations, their known enterprise or lack of it. Each family took pains to examine main and branches of family trees for any unfortunate signs of criminal records, traces of physical and other deformities. And if found, anything that could bring out the slightest frown on any face stopped discussions immediately. These included plain old laziness and suicide. As Esi's fathers and mothers reminded one another that Sunday afternoon, that was the only way to guarantee the health of future generations. They were ordering him to bring them solid people they could talk to or he might as well forget marrying their daughter.

Ali sat and listened polite-faced or repentant. When necessary he supplied answers in an 'I-too-can-play-a-very-good-boy' voice, as they queried, complained and scolded. So what else is new? he wondered. Nothing. North, south, east and west, clearly it was the same procedure everywhere. He only hoped that at the end of it all they would let him marry their daughter.

What Ali had told Esi's fathers about all his people being up north and therefore he not being able to produce anyone from his side was only half the truth. What he could not tell them was that he had not had the courage to ask any of his one or two close friends or his very distant relatives in Nima. He was convinced that none of his friends would want to have anything to do with the affair. He didn't have that many friends anyway, but of the few he had, he could not think of one who would willingly back him. Because, whether they were northern, southern, Muslim or Christian, one thing he sensed in all of them was an open respect and liking for Fusena. To an extent which sometimes made him feel a little jealous. As men they were all naturally engaged in different forms of 'away matches', as they self-indulgingly described their sexual adventures. But they also seemed to treat their wives with respect. A second wife? They wouldn't know how Fusena would take it. What they knew was how their wives would have taken it, in her place. And that was enough to advise them.

As for Ali's relatives in Nima, these were the various fathers,

104

mothers, brothers and sisters with whom his father had stayed on
his business trips to the south during the years he, Ali, was growing
up. So he knew them from when he was still young enough to go
around with his father. And over the years he had stayed in touch
with them. But life in Accra is full of mad and conflicting demands
on everyone, so he had not been able to give too much time to his
relationship with them. But people of his age or younger plainly
couldn't care. They too were into living their own lives and had
their own friends. And as for the older generation they understood.
After all, they could not have made the long, hard and often
humiliating journey from home to so far south without learning –
either because they had been old enough then or even as children
travelling with parents – that in this life, we often have to do what
is necessary and not what we would prefer. Even when they later
became big people in the community, and food and shelter ceased
to be daily burning issues, these were some of the lessons of life
they never, never forgot. And the result of all this was a general
understanding of other people's problems and a tolerance of their
shortcomings. For the patriarchs of Nima it was enough for them
that Musa's boy had grown up well. He had finished all his
education and even gone overseas and come back a decent young
man. Allah is great.

So when Ali went to tell his elders in Nima about his wanting to
marry Esi, the reaction he got shocked him. Contrary to all his
fears, no one raved about how a good Muslim boy would bring in
contamination in the form of a daughter of the infidels. No. What
they first fretted about was the fact that he had originally tried to
do the marrying behind their backs. They roundly scolded him for
that. Next, they asked him to look around properly. Hadn't they
all committed the crime he was also planning to be guilty of? Most
of them had married women of the south and daughters of the
infidels. It was survival. How can anyone go about, eating the
heads of cows, and also manage to maintain that he is afraid of
eyes? How could he be that hypocritical? Hmm? What really
surprised them was that a scholar of his standing and a modern
young man would want to have a second wife. They had thought
that such desires only lived in the breasts of people like them: old
and with only a few years of Koranic education. No, no, no. He

should not even try to tell them that he was not different from them. He was. They had no time to tell him how much. But the matter at hand was this business of his proposed second marriage. What was important was that if he kept it as a secret from his wife, it would be no marriage. Again if he just told his wife about it when it was already done or even before, but without her consent, it would be no marriage. Of course, no woman agreed to this sort of thing willingly. There was a time – maybe up to the days of their grandfathers – when women understood the necessity a little more. Since then, they have been understanding it less and less. Now, school or no school, no woman understands.

'So we have to work a little harder to convince them. But the convincing has to be done.' Ali would have to do things correctly, in the way they should be done. So to begin with, had he gained the consent of his wife?

The question hit Ali with the force of a fully loaded timber truck that was rolling down the Kwahu mountains towards Nkawkaw. He looked down. And since that was an even louder answer to their question than if he had spoken, the elders just went on to give the necessary advice. They wanted their son Ali to understand this clearly. They knew all this from experience. Of course, they would go with him to his new woman's people; to whatever hole they lived in. But not before Fusena agreed – however reluctantly. So he had better go tell her and come back to them. He could see them some other day. They were not going to disappear.

After all that, Ali looked so unhappy and so reluctant to get up and leave, his elders had to put their heads together and come up with some fresh ideas. And they did. They themselves would undertake the business of getting Fusena persuaded. Ali couldn't believe his ears or his luck. He literally jumped up, to shake their hands in gratitude.

Ali had not known it then, and was never to know, that in fact it was to these same elders that Fusena had gone to complain and to weep, the morning she drove so furiously from the house and later from the kiosk. So that the elders had just been biding their time, certain that their quarry would appear sooner or later.

A day or two after the meeting with Ali, the patriarchs of Nima had asked those among their wives and sisters whom they trusted had the patience and the wisdom to do the job properly, to talk to Fusena. The ladies had in turn sent a message to Fusena to come and see them. When they met, Fusena was quick to realise that if the men had asked the women to talk to her, then of course, they were not going to get Ali to give up the idea of marrying his graduate woman. She really could not believe that the beautiful journey that had began on the teacher training college campus was ending where it was threatening to. As she sat in front of the group of older women trying so diligently to listen to them, she knew that all was lost. Besides, what could she say to the good women, when some of them were themselves second, third and fourth wives? And those who had been first wives looked dignified, but clearly also so battle-weary? She decided to make their job easier for them.

'Yes, Mma. Yes, Auntie. Yes . . . yes . . . yes,' was all she said to every suggestion that was made. The older women felt bad. So an understanding that had never existed between them was now born. It was a man's world. You only survived if you knew how to live in it as a woman. What shocked the older women though, was obviously how little had changed for their daughters – school and all!

14

While Ali was trying to sort himself out in Accra, Esi had decided to go home one weekend and be with Ena her mother and Nana her grandmother. She had set out very early from the city and arrived to find them getting ready to go to church. So she was thinking that after the usual commotion that greeted her arrival had died down and everybody had gone she would just go and get some sleep. But that's not how things worked out. When her grandmother was all dressed in her starched cloth that made the most intriguing noises when she walked, she came to ask her, 'Please let us sit down, my lady.'

Esi's heart sank. She realised that her grandmother had decided that this was the morning to get some confessions out of her. And she was not going to wait until after the morning service was over. She was familiar with the line. So exactly what was it about Oko that repelled her so much, and what was it about Ali that attracted her? So far, she had succeeded in not yielding much at interrogations. Not because she hadn't thought those issues through. Deep down in her being, she feared that whatever her reasons were, they would not be considered respectable enough to tell anybody else about. But then, throughout her reasonably long life, Nana had never before given up on anything. She was determined to get something out of Esi, and this morning she did. Esi told her that Oko had been the only man in his home, or at least, one of the few men there. So there were too many women around him who did not like her. They hated her, she told the old lady. Who were these women, her grandmother wondered? According to Esi, it was his mother, his other mothers, his sisters.

What the old lady said:

'My young lady, today you came here asking me a question. I shall try as hard as possible to give you an answer. I shall also try to make it my truth, not anybody else's. For in a world where lies are pampered like the only children and nephews of queens and kings, all we can do is to hold on to our own truths. It used to be possible to talk and know that you and everyone else knew what you were talking about. It has stopped being like that for some time now. These days, we are getting used to people saying big things when they mean so little or nothing at all. They talk of pretty things when they intend ugly, and carry dangerous deeds home that properly belong to the bush.

'You are asking me whether you should marry this Ali of yours – who already has got his wife – and become one of his wives? Leave one man, marry another. What is the difference? Besides, you had a husband of your own, no? You had a husband of your own whom you have just left because you say he demanded too much of you and your time. But Esi tell me, doesn't a woman's time belong to a man? My lady Silk, that one is a very new and golden reason for leaving a man, if ever there was one, and if you are truly asking for my opinion. As for you and your stories, they cheer the heart of an old woman who has not found anything in this life amusing in a long time.

'Leave one man, marry another. Esi, you can. You have got your job. The government gives you a house. You have got your car. You have already got your daughter. You don't even have to prove you are a woman to any man, old or new. You can pick and choose. But remember, my lady, the best husband you can ever have is he who demands all of you and all of your time. Who is a good man if not the one who eats his wife completely, and pushes her down with a good gulp of alcohol? In our time, the best citizen was the man who swallowed more than one woman, and the more, the better. So our warriors and our kings married more women than other men in their communities. To prove that they were, by that single move, the best in the land.

'My lady Silk, remember a man always gained in stature through any way he chose to associate with a woman. And that included adultery. Especially adultery. Esi, a woman has always been diminished in her association with a man. A good woman was she who quickened the pace of her own destruction. To refuse, as a woman, to be destroyed, was a crime that society spotted very quickly and punished swiftly and severely.

'My lady Silk, it was not a question of this type of marriage or that type of marriage. It was not a question of being an only wife or being one of many wives. It was not being a wife here, there, yesterday or today. The product of the womb of my womb's product, it was just being a wife. It is being a woman. Esi, why do you think they took so much trouble with a girl on her wedding day? When we were young we were told that people who were condemned to death were granted any wish on the eve of their execution. By the way, was that ever true? Anyhow, a young woman on her wedding day was something like that. She was made much of, because that whole ceremony was a funeral of the self that could have been.

'In any case,' said Aanaa, 'I have had four children, and I know that each time a baby came out of me, I died a little. Somehow, my sister, there is a most minuscule fraction of time when the baby is tumbling out of her womb when the woman in labour dies.'

'Women die in too many ways anyway, my sister.

'They say it was not always like this. I mean about women and men. They say that a long time back, it was different. But it has been as it is for far too long for it to matter how it was in that far away yesterday. Besides, no one remembers what it was like then. Certainly from as long as even our ancestors may have been able to remember, it seemed to have always been necessary for women to be swallowed up in this way. For some reason, that was the only way societies were built, societies survived and societies prospered.

'That was the only way, my grandchild. Men were the first gods in the universe, and they were devouring gods. The only way they could yield their best – and sometimes their worst too – was if their egos were sacrificed to: regularly. The bloodier the sacrifice, the better. Oh yes. There are other types of gods. No less bloody, and equally implacable. We Africans have allowed ourselves to be regularly sacrificed to the egos of the Europeans, no? So that, among other things, they can build strong machines of fire to burn us all and then go to the moon . . . Ah, ah, ah, let me spit!

110

'Do I think it must always be so? Certainly not. It can be changed. It can be better. Life on this earth need not always be some humans being gods and others being sacrificial animals. Indeed, that can be changed. But it would take so much. No, not time. There has always been enough time for anything anyone ever really wanted to do. What it would take is a lot of thinking and a great deal of doing. But one wonders whether we are prepared to tire our minds and our bodies that much. Are we human beings even prepared to try?

'Otherwise, it is very possible for life on this earth to be good for us all. My lady Silk, everything is possible.'

'Aha?' Nana asked.

'Yes, Nana?'

'And your man from the Grasslands, doesn't he have sisters and mothers?'

Esi told her that to the best of her knowledge Ali had been an only child. No brothers. No sisters. The people from his extended family were far, far away. That was one main reason why she was thinking of agreeing to marry him. At that, Nana nearly fell off her short stool.

As for Esi's mother, she stood legs akimbo, stared hard at Esi and called her a witch. 'How can I call you my daughter when you hate people?'

'Ena, I don't hate people. It is just that . . .'

The two older women would not even let her continue. Why? Destroy a perfectly good marriage because your husband has too many people around him? Ei. In the old days wasn't that one of the big reasons why any family gave their princess to any man in marriage? And how can you tell yourself you like some man because you don't know a single relative of his? Ei. But wasn't that a good reason to avoid a man in the old days?

'So tell me, my lady,' said Nana very seriously and slowly, 'if you are with your man of the Grasslands and something happened to him whom would you run to?

Esi too thought about the question, and brought out a reply.

'Nana,' she began, 'when he comes here to ask for my hand, he would have to bring somebody. This is the custom, no?'

Nana nodded her head.

'Nana,' Esi continued with her answer, 'whoever he brings with him then, to meet you and my fathers, it would be that person I shall run to, if I'm with Ali and something happened to him.' It had been a rather cool reply; the social scientist and statistican speaking.

Esi's mother murmured, 'Ei, Esi,' and ran off. Her grandmother hadn't exclaimed. In fact, she was silently pleased at the sharpness of her granddaughter's mind, and deliberately allowed herself to be overcome by the new wisdom of a young woman who had let herself get well into booklearning.

When the older women left for church, Esi remained in her grandmother's chamber. At first she sat in a chair for a long time; she had to admit that she was suffering from a mixture of emotional and physical exhaustion. So she gave up thinking, went to lie down on her grandmother's bed and fell into a deep sleep.

She slept for a long time during which her mother and grandmother must have returned from church, and even got some food ready. She had not heard a thing. And now as she struggled awake, she could hear voices.

Ena:	What shall we tell the child?
Nana:	You have already made a mistake.
Ena:	What mistake?
Nana:	By calling her a child.
Ena:	And isn't she my daughter?
Nana:	That she is.
Ena:	So then, what crime do I commit if –?
Nana:	Please, select your words very carefully. Your daughter – my granddaughter – has thrown a problem at us. That is what we are talking about. Committing crimes should not even be mentioned here.
Ena:	But Mother –
Nana:	What? Now don't you dare turn into a child and melt on me. You should know by now that I do not approve of many things these days. Like many ways of behaving and speaking. Not because they are new and I'm old, but because they are just bad.

Ena: Mother!

Nana: You shut up. Since you have already called your daughter a child, and you are my daughter, maybe I should call you a child and treat you like one. (She pauses.) Listen, you gave birth to Esi. But when was the last time you wiped any shit off her bottom? (The mother is stunned. She looks at the older woman, her own mother, as if waiting for an answer to the question from her. And she gets it.)

Nana: You have nothing to say, or you can't remember? Well, that's how old she is. She is a woman. And remember that after you have called someone a child, there is nothing you can tell her which she is going to find useful.

Ena: You see, that's what I meant.

Nana: What did you mean?

Ena: I meant: look at my life. It hasn't been much of anything. What can I take out of such a life and give to anybody? Even if she is my own child? And Esi had such high school education and she is such a big lady.

Nana: Have I not asked you to shut up? Especially if you are going to utter such stupidities. I wonder what has come over you these days. (Musingly) I wonder how it escaped me.

Ena: What escaped you?

Nana: That you were growing into a fool.

Ena: Oh Mother!

Nana: Yes, you have grown up very badly.

Ena: Why are you saying all these harsh things to me?

Nana: Because my daughter, it is not our fault that you and I did not go to school. I can also forgive myself and you that we have not made money . . . Even not having more than one child is not so bad . . .

Ena: After all, some have none at all.

Nana: Indeed, some have none at all.

Ena and Nana: But only fools pity themselves.

Nana: Eheh!

Ena:	And no one forgives fools.
Nana:	Eyiwaa.
Ena:	Not even themselves.
Nana:	Thank you!

From the inner room Esi heard them and pain filled her chest. She could never be as close to her mother as her mother was to her grandmother. Never, never, never. And she knew why. Not that knowing exactly why helped much. Trying to ward off despair was proving difficult. She could only ask the emptiness a few questions.

Why had they sent her to school?

What had they hoped to gain from it?

What had they hoped she would gain from it?

Who had designed the educational system that had produced her sort?

What had that person or those people hoped to gain from it?

For surely, taking a ten-year-old child away from her mother, and away from her first language – which is surely one of life's most powerful working tools – for what would turn out to be forever, then transferring her into a boarding school for two years, to a higher boarding school for seven years, then to an even higher boarding school for three or four years, from where she was only equipped to go and roam in strange and foreign lands with no hope of ever meaningfully re-entering her mother's world . . . all this was too high a price to pay to achieve the dangerous confusion she was now in and the country now was in.

She tried to suppress a cough and could not. Her mother and grandmother heard her.

From the outer room, the grandmother's voice came, full of love and strong with concern, 'My lady, my lady . . .'

'Yes, Nana,' Esi replied, struggling for an equally strong voice.

'When you are ready you can join us here,' the grandmother continued.

'Yes Nana,' replied Esi, jumping up. She knew that although it had been put to her very nicely in the form of a request, her grandmother's words were a command. As she walked the few paces between them and her, her mood changed again. As a young

Ghanaian woman government statistician divorcee, a mother of one child, getting ready to be a second wife and the rest, she was aware of these and other equally serious personal, and not so personal, questions. But she was also going to be humble enough to admit that the answers to them could not come from her, an individual. Hopefully a whole people would soon have answers for them. In the meantime she would listen to her grandmother. She would not pity herself. She would just relax and flourish in her mother's and her grandmother's peace.

The second time that Ali went to Esi's village was the Sunday that began the last quarter of the year. This time he took his elders with him and Esi's fathers did not ask him how he had managed to produce such solid people after all. Everybody just saw to it that everything went smoothly. When the necessary questions were asked, they received appropriate replies. So kola was broken and gin was poured in libation and a little of it drunk by Esi's people. Ali and his people, as practising Muslims, could not share the alcohol. Esi's fathers ritualistically asked for, and were given by Ali's people, the very small sum that symbolised dowry.

Finally, Ali gave a pure gold ring to one of the women to be given to Esi. And if any of the people around were surprised, they didn't show it. After all, everyone knew that both Esi and Ali were 'scholars' for whom, naturally, the white man's customs were considered very important. All the spirits should have been appeased: ancient coastal and Christian, ancient northern and Islamic, the ghost of the colonisers.

At that stage, everyone knew that the purpose of all the weeks of discussions and the goings and comings had been served. Esi and Ali had become man and wife. Some of the women raised ululations. Even children joined in. Everyone was happy. There was some eating and drinking. For such an occasion, Esi a divorcee and Ali already having a wife, no one expected a huge wedding ceremony or celebration. Not even in the best of circumstances.

Before they left Esi's village in their separate cars that Sunday, Ali and Esi had agreed that he would be waiting at her house for her. After all, he had a bunch of duplicate keys to the gate, the main front door and indeed, the whole house. Therefore she could not

115

believe her eyes that when she arrived he was not in the house. There was not a soul in the house, and her feeling of disappointment was sharp. What she couldn't understand though was that any area of her mind could have expected anyone else apart from Ali. There couldn't have been. And as for her newly-acquired husband, he was probably home with his wife and children, to whom it must seem that he had been away from home too often for too long lately. It occurred to Esi that if Ali had told Fusena where he was bound for when he set out earlier that morning, then there would be no need for him to hide anything. And late as it was, he could still drop by her place for a little while at least? But if he had not told her, then of course it was going to be difficult for him to find another excuse to be out of their house again in the evening of the same day, much of which he had spent with her and her people. Then she told herself it was silly to speculate. She unpacked her car. She nearly gave in to a temptation to leave the gate open. But she gathered some courage to go out and lock it. She also locked the car up, went inside and locked the front door behind her.

The sun set completely and Ali did not come. Esi admitted that she was feeling rather depressed. Soon after watching the news, she went and had a bath and changed into night clothes. There had been quite a lot of eating back in the village and although she couldn't recall sitting herself down to have a proper meal, she knew she had nibbled a lot. In any case, it was not a question of how much she had eaten earlier in the day. She had no appetite for food. She decided to go to bed early. After all, the next day was a regular working day.

Lying alone in bed with her eyes hard and wide-open in the dark, she remembered some of the advice her mother and her grandmother had given her. They had told her to be careful. That being one of any number of wives had its rules. If she obeyed the rules, a woman like her should be all right. If she broke the rules, then her new marriage would be like a fire that had been lighted inside her. They recited some of the rules to her. They made her aware of some of the pitfalls. Above all, they said, there were two things she had to bear in mind at all times. One was never to forget that she was number two, and the other was never to show jealousy. She almost started laughing. It had not even taken half of one day for her to begin to know what being number two meant, had it?

And as for not showing jealousy, how did anyone begin to do that? Suddenly, she started remembering something else: her marriage to Oko and especially her wedding day. On that day, the problem had been how to find a minute and a corner to herself. She had later realised that as a bride, in fact, she had not been expected to be alone at all. And she had not been. Not at that day's beginning, and definitely not at its end.

'Oh well,' she yielded to the night and the dark, and drifted off to sleep.

15

Ali could already see his house when he decided to go back to Esi. He had been feeling guilty for all the fifteen or so minutes since he'd left her. Of course, there had been no question of sleeping at hers tonight; tonight being New Year's Eve. Although Muslims, and therefore he and Fusena had very little interest in Christmas, they could never avoid the general air of festivity that simply invaded everything and everywhere around this time of the year. Like other Muslims, Ali felt particularly bitter about the fact that the country didn't bother to claim a state religion, yet Christianity was everywhere. Assumed. The children were especially vulnerable. Towards the end of the year, which was also the end of the first school term, they always came home singing Christmas carols. He and Fusena had still not got an answer to the problem. So they bought the children some balloons and sweets and soft drinks. New clothes were still only for the Id. And no expensive Christmas presents either. That would be going too far. Altogether the struggle to maintain a difference between Christmas and Islamic festivals was extremely difficult.

New Year was different. He and Fusena had, over the years, established a pattern for New Year. He organised his business affairs in such a way that he wouldn't have to be away from home on New Year's Eve and New Year's Day. On New Year's Eve, he dropped everything by six o'clock if it had been a working day, and went home. He was convinced that a man had to see his family – at least for a while – by the daylight of the passing old year, and let the family see him. Not that once he was home, they did anything special. They just had *tuo* together. Then when the children were asleep, he and Fusena would sit and watch whatever was on television. Depending on how they felt, they talked or sat in a relaxed friendly silence. In recent years, he would sometimes select a film he knew both he and Fusena would enjoy, and show it on video. When the new year actually arrived, he would open a bottle of champagne, and they'd each have a glass – the only time he shared alcohol with Fusena. Then they would wish one another a happy New Year, then go to bed, make love and sleep. On the New Year's Day they had an open house. Nothing like a conscious celebration. But there would be kola, fried meat, gravy and rice. And lots of fruits, for themselves and any friends that cared to drop in. For something to drink there would be non-alcoholic beverages for strict Muslims, and different alcohols for anyone else who preferred them. It was often a pleasantly loose day: the kind he enjoyed tremendously because most of his days were really so unhealthily busy. So they spent New Year's Day very much like they did the last day of Id: let it assume its own character and momentum.

Now here he was: one part of him feeling the need to hurry home and initiate known rituals, while another part of him was busy feeling guilty.

Guilty in spite of the fact that by all the precepts of his upbringing Esi was indeed his wife, and yet by 'home' he meant only one place, which was where Fusena and his children were. Hopelessly guilty because he knew that there was not the slightest possibility of him ever being able to establish any rituals in the relationship with Esi.

However, on this particular afternoon, he decided, there was something he could do. It wouldn't be much, but it would be something. From the office, where he was, he would go and spend some more time with her, and then he would rush home. It was already getting to five o'clock, and it was plain that he would not be able to make his six o'clock deadline. A real pity. However, he would try and be there before the children had to go to bed. In a flash, he had jumped into his car and was heading towards Esi's place.

How did our fathers manage? He wondered to himself. He knew the answer. They, our fathers, lived in a world which was ordered to make such arrangements work. For instance, no man in the old days would be caught in his present predicament: that is, wondering which woman he would be making love to on a New Year's Eve.

That was the real problem this afternoon, he admitted to himself. And the thought panicked him so much that he nearly hit a young girl who was crossing the street holding the hands of a little boy who must have been her brother. He screeched to a stop, his heart thumping very badly. He drove the car to the side of the road to enable him to pull himself together. Then he looked across the street and saw the girl and the little boy hopping along their way as if nothing had happened. He sighed with relief. He started the car and decided almost at the same time that he would go back to the office and pick up a bottle of champagne for Esi.

Esi was very surprised and pleased to see him. Yet after managing a rather muted hello she said almost nothing at all, all the time she was opening the gate and entering the house with him. And he didn't say anything. They just went to her bedroom, and started eating one another up. It was a wild and desperate lovemaking. For both of them. For Esi it was shame for her dependence on a man who, as far as she could see, was too preoccupied with other matters to ever be with her . . . and of course for him it was several shades of guilt, especially one which was a product of an awareness that if he was so busy pumping into Esi, then he was also busy ruining a tradition. And the more he thought of what he was destroying between him and Fusena, the more his groins burned, and the harder he drove into Esi. And both he and Esi peaked so high, they feared they wouldn't survive that incredible climax. Then he was ready to empty some of his confusion and genuine affection for both women into a cauldron that was one.

Just at that moment they heard a car come through the gate. They couldn't believe their ears. But sure enough it was a car, and they could hear it parking outside where their two cars were. Their passion died instantly, each pair of eyes asking the other who they thought it could be. Esi remembered with regret that in her excitement at seeing Ali again she had not locked the main gate or any of the doors after Ali had come in. There was nothing she could do about any of that now. There was knocking on the front door . . . Poom, poom, poom. 'Esi . . .' Poom, poom, poom, poom. 'Esi . . .?'

Ali got off from on top of Esi and fell on the bed beside her. Whoever it was had tried the front door, found it unlocked and was in the front room already.

'Esi, Esi, Esi.'

Then Esi knew who the voice belonged to. It was Oko's voice. Esi jumped off the bed, naked like the day she was born, rushed to the door between the bedroom and sitting-room, banged it shut and double-locked it. Ali was never to forget that. Because he just couldn't figure out how anyone can have that much presence of mind in the middle of a crisis. But then having done that, neither Esi herself nor Ali knew what to do next. And of course, they couldn't discuss the situation.

In the meantime, Oko must have realised what was happening when Esi locked the door, and now even more angry with himself for not rushing straight into the bedroom in the first place, he was banging on the door and calling her name with a frenzy which Esi was later to think had been amusingly childish. But of course at the time, she had been in no position to laugh.

'I know you are in there, so why don't you answer?' he was screaming. Esi's mouth refused to open up. Finally, she and Ali got up at the same time, and hurriedly put their clothes on. Then, opening the door only wide enough for his slim body to pass through, Ali went out. When Oko saw him, he dashed towards the door, as if to rush in. But the door had a Yale lock and Ali quickly banged it shut and locked both of them out of the bedroom. Frustrated, Oko turned and faced Ali.

'Where is she?' he demanded.

'Where is who?' Ali asked coolly, as if he genuinely had not the slightest idea to whom the other man was referring.

'My wife,' Oko thundered.

'Your what?' Ali demanded.

'My wife. That's what I said, and you heard me well,' said Oko.

'Your wife?' and Ali burst out laughing. Oko got hold of the front of Ali's shirt.

'Yes, yes,' Oko screamed again, 'the bitch you have been

sleeping with. She is my wife.' He was shaking with rage, as he tried to shake Ali.

To break free, Ali pushed Oko away from him so violently, Oko virtually fell. He didn't quite, but a button from his shirt fell to the floor.

Then a child began to cry. It was Ogyaanowa. Oko picked himself up quickly and resumed banging on the door. Ogyaanowa continued yelling. Ali was trying to prise him away from the bedroom door and saying over and over and over, almost to himself, 'Listen, I don't know who you are, but Esi is my wife . . . I don't know who you are, but Esi is my wife . . . I don't know . . .'

Oko left the door, turned on Ali with a raised fist. But Ali was too quick for him. He got hold of the raised hand. Then, as they began to struggle, Esi, who had heard Ogyaanowa from the bedroom, opened the door, rushed out, passed the two men, picked up the child, ran with her into her car and drove off. She left two very surprised men staring after the car.

16

Opokuya was feeling sorry for herself and tired. Tired from being too conscientious. Tired of being too mindful of other people's needs and almost totally ignoring her own. Tired from having to be in too many places at the same time. First, and as usual, there was the hospital. For one more end-of-the-year season, she had not been able to give herself any 'offs'. However desperate she may have felt, she kept telling herself that it just wasn't right that she who fixed the rota should also give herself the best part of the timetable; like going off during the Christmas and New Year holidays. Practically everyone else wanted to go off around that time. Obviously, when the ancients had said that 'who shares the meat doesn't eat bones,' they hadn't counted people with her kind of conscience, had they?

So there she was, administering the hospital and delivering babies on New Year's Eve! And for the dozenth time and year, whenever she felt free for a minute, she would look at the calendar behind her chair and try to focus on the month of April.

'What is so peculiar about April? Could one be right in thinking that people actually plan to get pregnant in April so that they would have Christmas babies?' Of course, the Easter holidays were nearly always in April. 'Well, well, well,' she murmured to herself. Christianity had her firmly by the throat. However, she also told herself that in fact, people might not be having more babies at the end of the year than in any given number of days during the rest of the year. That it probably was just that precisely because of the season, and with other people so busy having a nice time, it always seemed as if those who had to work had more to do than normal. Besides, Christmas and New Year births turned out to be even more of social occasions than normal. Families and friends had more time to visit, and stay around and carry on. And again because of the general festive atmosphere, one tended to be more lenient with visitors who then exploited all this to take pictures of newborns and their mothers, open bottles of champagne if they were of the champagne-popping kind, and literally throw parties in the wards. It all boiled down to more work for hospital staff.

She had definitely worked throughout the holidays, but she had also planned this last day of the year to go straight home from the hospital to cook for New Year's Day. She would make a big pot of *abe nkwan* and an equally big pot of *jolof* rice. And of course, bowls of chips. That way, the family could nibble, and still have regular meals with enough food left over for visiting members of the extended family and friends.

But things hadn't gone too well this afternoon. Only the pot of soup was safely simmering away. The chips seemed to disappear through the bottom of the bowl, like the water which the poor dwarf was supposed to fill the basket with. Except that this time, red-blooded human children kept stealing them of course. Eventually, Opokuya had decided to make the cat feel responsible for the safety of the fish. She had told Nana Aba, her oldest child, that she was leaving the whole affair to her and Dada, the older of her two sons. They knew the recipe. They had better fill the bowl with chips themselves . . .

As for the *jolof* rice, it had met with a major accident. As soon as it had started to give off its aromas, a whole load of Kubi's young relatives had arrived. And right now they were sitting around the dining table, busy chomping away. How was she going to cope? Stay up and cook again? Sneak off to bed early enough so that she could wake up early to cook another pot before going to the hospital?

'Mama . . . Mama . . .' That was Kweku's voice and fists on the door. The door opened before she could ask him to come in.

'Mama, Mama.'

'What is it?'

'Auntie Esi is here.' The information was accompanied with audible panting from the excitement of it all.

'Auntie Esi? Esi, here?' Opokuya herself was almost dazed with surprise.

'She has come. And Ogyaanowa too,' Kweku announced. Opokuya jumped up. She adjusted her headscarf. But before she could open the door to go out, Esi entered.

'Es . . .' Opokua had wanted to ask, 'how come you are here?' or something like that. Instead, she had a good look at Esi's face and immediately asked Kweku to take Ogyaanowa to the kitchen where all the young people were.

'Tell Nana Aba to look after her . . . They must give her plenty of chips, you hear?' she called after the retreating backs of the two children.

Then she shut the door.

'Esi, what is it?'

'Oko and Ali are fighting,' Esi blurted out.

Opokuya nearly laughed. But she checked herself. Later, she knew the two of them would holler over the incident together. But now it would just be unfair to Esi. The fact that people are our friends doesn't mean we can be rude or unkind to them. So she just motioned Esi to sit on the bed, and sat by her. Since nothing occurred to her which she wanted to voice out, she kept quiet and gently rocked her friend as though Esi was a baby.

After a while, Esi looked up at Opokuya and they both smiled. When Esi began to tell her story, Opokuya asked her to wait. She ran out of the bedroom and into the front room to bring Kubi. As Kubi entered the bedroom he murmured a rather cold greeting, then stood by a window, heavy as a cloud, while Esi told her story. For nearly half an hour, Esi spoke without interruption. Opokuya and Kubi just exclaimed every now and then: 'Christ', 'Lord' and 'Good Lord', and others in that vein.

After she had finished, the first thing that Kubi asked was, 'So you left them there fighting?'

'Yes,' Esi said, already feeling scolded.

'Well, it is extremely dangerous, isn't it? One never knows what they might do to one another.'

'But Kubi, there was very little Esi could have done, really. She could not have separated them even if she had stayed on. And in any case, it wouldn't have been wise to let Ogyaanowa see more of the fighting.'

'I believe you are right,' Opokuya's husband agreed grudgingly. Then he announced that he would go to Esi's house and check on those two anyway.

After he had found the keys to their car and was going out, Opokuya asked him to take one or two of the eldest of his visiting nephews with him. And please, could he be careful and remember it was the eve of a new year?

17

When Kubi and his nephews got to Esi's place, they found the gate wide open, and so they drove in. The door of the house was locked though. Clearly, Oko and Ali were both gone. Kubi suggested that they should walk around the house to see if everything was all right. This was fairly difficult to do because it was already dark and there were no lights on, either outside or inside the house. Kubi remembered he had a torch in the glove compartment of his car. One of the young men fetched it and they began to do the inspection as best as they could. Two windows were open in the sitting room, and one in the main bedroom. They manoeuvred them to get them to appear shut. When they were as satisfied as the situation permitted, they drove out and parked the car outside the gate. Then they went back to the gate, and removed the padlock since they weren't sure that Esi had taken its key with her when she was leaving. Finally, they looked for and found a piece of wire. They wired the gate shut, and drove to Sweet Breezes Hill.

As soon as they arrived, Kubi went straight to the kitchen where he'd expected to find the two women. They were there with the children. He called them back into the bedroom, and gave them a report, using his best civil service voice. During his narration, Esi realised that she was close to tears. But she told herself silently that she was not the tearful type, so she had better pull herself together.

The three of them discussed the situation at length. They speculated on what could have happened at her place after she left. They came to a rather reassuring conclusion that, from the way the place looked, each of the men must have driven away in his own car.

Then they moved to wondering whether Kubi should not drive

over to Oko's mother to check on Oko. At first, Esi wouldn't hear of it. She knew that if he saw Kubi, Oko would want to come back with him to collect Ogyaanowa. Kubi was insistent because he too was convinced that it was his responsibility to check on his friend. During the exchange, quite a bit of the bad feeling that had accumulated between him and Esi surfaced. Opokuya stood by and silently suffered. She was convinced that even though her friend may have been partly responsible for the way things had turned out, Kubi was also being terribly unfair. However, she couldn't say any of this openly.

In the end, Kubi left the two women and drove to Oko's mother's house. Oko was there – with a cut lip. Kubi found this so funny, he laughed out loud as the two of them split a beer and Oko winced each time he raised the glass to his lips. He related his version of what had happened.

'Of course, legally, you are in the wrong,' Kubi ventured. Oko glared rather fiercely at him. Kubi took the hint and didn't continue with that line of discussion. After all, he had not come to rub salt into his friend's wound. And besides, he knew too well that our passions do not always meet at the same junction with the points of the law.

An hour or so later, Kubi informed Oko that it was time he went back to Sweet Breezes Hill.

'I'll follow you in my car then,' Oko announced.

'What for?'

'I'm coming for my daughter.'

Kubi was plainly distressed. Of course Esi had been right. Anyway, one thing he was perfectly clear about that night was that he was not returning home with Oko trailing behind him. He tried to reason the issue out: that it was too late; that it was a special evening; that there had been enough commotion already for the child without having to drag her across the streets of Accra on a night like that.

'Wasn't her mother aware of all that when she went whoring on the last day of the year? . . . Eh, my friend?' Oko asked Kubi with a dead-pan face.

Kubi didn't respond to that. What good would it do to remind an angry man that strictly speaking Esi must have been sleeping quite willingly with a man who had married her, and that that could not be remotely described as whoring. He saw his main task then as seeing to it that Oko stayed well and calm where he was, and Ogyaanowa left alone. And clearly, he would achieve neither by trying to argue with the man. Eventually he succeeded by sitting quietly and drinking his beer. Besides, for all his fury and bravado, it was apparent that Oko was tired.

When Kubi finally got up to leave, Oko's mother came to express her thanks to him, and saw to it that she did not miss the opportunity to ask him whether 'our master knew the kind of drug which a woman like that gangling witch could have given an honourable man like my son to behave so oddly? Because,' she went on, doing her own little shouting into the night, 'there must be something really wrong when a man decides to go and fight another man over a woman who has treated him as shabbily as that woman has treated Oko . . . Don't you think so, my master?'

Kubi knew that he was not really expected to say anything, and so he said nothing, except something very polite like, 'Mama, all will be well in the end,' and 'perhaps things might be better in the New Year.' Then he said his farewells with a promise to come the next day to see Oko. They wished one another A Happy Meeting of the Years, and Kubi drove away.

Esi and her daughter Ogyaanowa spent the rest of that night with Opokuya and her family. For Ogyaanowa, and Opokuya's children, the whole episode seemed to have added something unexpected and therefore exciting. Before the young people went to bed, they had made more chips than the bowlful Opokuya had asked them to. Their lot was not anywhere as fine as the lot Opokuya had made earlier. But then, only 'Mama' could tell the difference.

For Opokuya herself, Esi's invasion had been a real boon. Each time Kubi had left, they had stayed in the bedroom talking for a little while longer; then they had moved to the kitchen where, chatting and laughing as the two of them continuously did whenever they were together, Opokuya not only made an equally huge pot of *jolof* rice, but Esi too fried lots of fish and prawns. Indeed, by midnight, Opokuya was convinced that she could feed all of the king's workmen if necessary. At midnight they had joined

Kubi in the sitting room and wished one another a Happy New Year and had a drink. The kids were already in bed. Then the grown-ups stayed up for a while chatting about this and that. Finally, it was agreed that Kubi would find himself somewhere to sleep and therefore Esi could share the bedroom with Opokuya for the rest of the night.

It was already two o'clock in the morning. Plainly for Opokuya there wasn't much of the night left. She had to wake up at five – exactly three hours later – to get ready for the hospital. When she stepped down from the bed, she could hardly walk for fatigue. One consolation was that at least there was food for everyone in the house, and more.

Esi spent the rest of the New Year holidays at Opokuya's. She had wanted to return to her place the next day, although she had waited for Opokuya to come home from the hospital before doing so. But both Opokuya and Kubi cautioned her against returning so soon. They all knew that Oko was not a violent man, but then they also agreed that you never knew what anybody can do when he is feeling angry and hurt. Besides, said Opokuya, why leave the house where there were quite a few children for Ogyaanowa to play with and return her where there wasn't a single other child? So, with her mind's eye Esi looked at her bungalow and surveyed the entire neighbourhood. Most families would have gone away anyway, and the whole place would be silent in a way which she would not mind but which she also had to admit could be oppressive for a child. So she agreed they would stay, although she insisted that she should dash back to the place to double-check on the doors and the windows and also bring more clothes for herself and Ogyaanowa.

From Esi's house, Ali had driven back to his office to sit there and calm his nerves. He told himself that it just wouldn't do for him to get back to Fusena and the children looking visibly shaken or in any shape that would prompt them to ask questions. Once in the office, he had taken a bottle of mineral water from the fridge and had had a good drink. A few minutes later, and feeling somewhat collected, he had phoned home. Fusena was almost incoherent with concern. Where was he? Was he all right? He had assured her repeatedly. When she mentioned that they had been waiting for him to come home so that they could all eat supper together, he felt really bad. But he asked her to eat with the children. She would not agree. How could he expect her to? Eventually, he persuaded her to let the children eat so that they could go to bed. She agreed to that, but she would wait for him, of course . . .

Having sorted that out for the meantime – and he was aware it was only for the meantime – he turned his attention back to Esi. Because he had no doubt that that was where they would go, he phoned the Dakwas' to make sure that she and Ogyaanowa were safe. Of course they were there. He had been passed on to Esi almost immediately, and he had virtually crooned to her, apologising for his contribution to the embarrassment she had suffered. Esi had in turn said that frankly she did not know what he was talking about. It was she who had to apologise. After all, it was her ex-husband who had come to embarrass them all. Wasn't it?

'Okay, okay, but I am feeling bad all the same.'

'Were you hurt, Ali?'

'No . . . no,' said Ali, making clicking noises to show his disapproval for the way she seemed to be so concerned about him. Although deep down he could not help feeling pleased too. It was at the end of the telephone conversation that he also suggested to Esi that she stay away from her bungalow for a day or two.

On the second day of January, which was a Friday, Ali drove to the Dakwa house with a bottle of whisky and one of gin for Kubi and Opokuya, and a carload of goodies calculated to win young hearts forever. They were meant for Ogyaanowa and the two youngest Dakwa children. Toffees, other sweets, cakes, balloons, sodas. Even toys. The kids were very happy with everything. The grown-ups not so much. Kubi hardly looked at him although he managed to do what was expected, including offering Ali a drink. Ali declined alcohol in favour of some fruit juice. As for the children, they destroyed the ears of the grown-ups with non-stop choruses of how very very nice they thought 'Uncle Ali' was.

In the meantime, Oko had decided that behaving the way he had just done wouldn't do. It was a definite lowering of standards. Why make that bitch think she was the only woman in the world? He was going to leave her and get on with his life. Before he returned to his secondary school, he took one male relative with him and they went to Esi's house to collect the child. Ogyaanowa was thoroughly fed up with having no one else around apart from the housekeeper when her mother went to work. So when she saw her father, she showed such an eagerness to go with him, Esi really felt rejected. But she let the child go anyway.

18

Half way through the new year, Ali took Esi to Bamako; but not before he had sent messages ahead to warn his people. That is, Mma, Baba Danjuma, and his natural father, Musa Musa. This was his 'real' family and separate from the 'Nima' family. The latter, was, in reality, only a support system in an alien environment. He had been very careful with the message. It contained among others an apology for the fact that he had not been able to obtain their permission before taking up a second wife.

Ali knew very well that in the old days, his behaviour would have been unthinkable, and definitely unforgivable. For no matter how old you were or felt, you could not get married without your parents knowledge. And your parents were

the father who helped your mother to conceive you,
the mother who gave birth to you,
and all those who claimed to be brothers and
sisters to those two.

Like all 'modern Western-educated Africans', Ali couldn't help it if he regularly bruised traditions and hurt people. But at least he was one of the few really sensitive ones. So he went home to Bamako, armed with plenty of real and symbolic kolas to say he was sorry.

It was already sundown when Ali and Esi arrived in Bamako, so there was very little talk. What there was, was not serious. Mma just saw to it that the travellers were comfortable for the night, so they got water to wash, a very light meal, a place to sleep. Ali had asked his office to book them into the most modern hotel in town for the duration of their stay. But he realised that at least for that night he was in no position to insist on not staying at Mma's. It would not have been right at all. There was plenty of time to sort out the question of independent accommodation as well as other matters the next day. So for that night they slept at Mma's.

In the light of an open day, Mma looked Esi over. She found her beautiful. But she also decided that Esi was not someone she would ever be able to warm to. She knew Fusena, liked her very much and approved enormously of her as a wife for her son. Besides, she would always remember the trouble she had had to go to in order to get Fusena as a wife for Ali. That sort of situation inevitably got you attached to people even if the lines of your lives never really allow you to get ever very close to them.

On the other hand, she told herself, her son Ali was not a fool. He had worked well and made something of himself. He had prospered. And as a son, he showed in every way that he cared for his family and for her in particular. Not only had he been helping her and Baba Danjuma to educate the younger children as if there were no difference between him and the others; in fact, it was clear that his office in Bamako had been given permanent instructions to make regular remittances to them. Yes, Ali had not forgotten his beginnings . . . So, if he found a woman like Esi attractive enough to want to marry her, then that should be good enough for her. He could have organised the matter of the permission better. But then, the joy of having children is also sometimes having to forgive them when, after they had done wrong, they come back to say sorry.

Musa Musa put up a different show altogether. He ranted and raved openly against the couple, telling Ali that he should be ashamed of himself. And that, as far as he was concerned, Esi was still just a concubine.

'Because you had not bothered either to bring her to introduce her to us, or to get our approval before entering into this so-called marriage. It was not enough to ask your relatives from Nima along to your new in-laws. Besides, Allah is our witness, what else is the daughter of an infidel good for besides concubinage? Eh?

. . . Are good Muslim women finished from the earth? . . . And talking of good Muslim women, by the way, where is Fusena? Why don't you make it possible for me to see my grandchildren more often? Eh, Ali? I have only seen them once since you all arrived from the white man's land . . . And my last grandchild, never. Allah, what tribulations people expect me to suffer! –'

Ali tried to stop his father and refresh his memory about how only recently he had been with them in Accra. But Musa Musa was not going to allow any such interruption.

'– Yes, so w-h-e-r-e is Fusena? Eh, Ali? And what does taking a second wife mean? What tasks had you given her to perform for which her energies had seemed inadequate? Eh, Ali? And how has she felt about all this?'

Eventually, Mma found herself helping Ali to beg for forgiveness. When Musa Musa was somewhat mollified, he chatted easily to Esi and openly flirted with her.

> This was traditionally permitted and sometimes even expected, when the relationship between a woman and her father-in-law was good. As long as it did not go beyond the level of a harmless game.

For an incurable womaniser like Musa Musa, there was always a threat of any harmless flirtations becoming serious. But after his eyes had raked Esi's body and he had in fact concluded that he could sleep with her, he had made a decision not to do anything 'disgraceful'. He had told himself that he didn't believe in older men like him acting as though their sons were their procurers, hiding behind bushes to steal their children's prey. As he grew older, his motto had been that the day he stopped attracting women for himself, that was also the day he gave up women! Therefore, he decisively instructed himself that Esi was forbidden territory.

After the initial difficulties with Ali's family, Esi had had a lovely time in Bamako. She liked Ali's people. She liked Mma, although she also found her a little intimidating. On the other hand, from the first moment of encounter she had found Musa Musa charming and had not allowed herself to be remotely deceived by his earlier show of disapproval. She couldn't get close enough to Baba Danjuma even to form an opinion about him. But that too was all right. It is known and accepted that some relationships by marriage are really too distant to grow much.

Like anyone from the coast, meat had always been a luxury for

Esi. In Bamako she ate enough during those two weeks to last her a very long time. What she couldn't get over though, were the chickens and guinea fowls, succulently smoked with wild mint and other bewitchingly subtle flavours. It occurred to her then that perhaps when the best of African pastoral and campsite cooking met French cooking, you got *pintade fumée avec vin blanc sec. Trop sec.* She indulged.

Ali had been fascinated, watching Esi as she made some genuine efforts to operate in his other environment. For, apart from creating situations in which she could use the few words and phrases of French she knew, she had also started to learn Hausa, which is the *lingua franca* of the Sub-Sahel. At the end of the two weeks they turned their eyes southwards, loaded with all manner of goodies: Sub-Sahelian African as well as French, as well as nearly five kilos of extra body weight on Esi. And with all that was a conviction shared by both that they had had a wonderful holiday.

Part III

19

'Okay, if you can wait for a couple of minutes I could drop you home.

'Hello, yes . . . hello, yes, yes, yes, it's Ali . . . Hi . . . yes. Oh, but I have missed you! Fine, fine. And how are you?

'Yes, oh yes. About four o'clock this afternoon.

'Yes, fine.

'Okay. But exhausting as usual . . .

'Yes, this time, properly worn out . . .

'Eh . . . eh . . I . . . well . . . eh . . . actually I am going straight home to wash out all this travel dirt . . . and . . . nothing at all. Just jump into bed to try and recover from my jet-lag . . .

'Esi, please try to understand . . .

'Darling, it's not like you to be unreasonable . . .

'Not today.

'Because it's never possible for me to breeze through your place for five minutes . . . please?

'Yes, tomorrow evening.

'Oh, definitely, I shall come straight from work. So how about cooking me one of your specialities?

'Ya . . . Ya . . . Ya . . . Ya . . .

' . . . Good . . .

' . . . Lovely . . .

' . . . See you then. Okay . . . Bye!

Fade in the end-of-day sounds of the city and its traffic: yes, do fade them in: especially when you are in doubt.

It was now nearly a year since Esi remarried, and she was settled into her new life. In all, her basic hopes for marrying a man like Ali had been fulfilled. Ali was not on her back every one of every twenty-four hours of every day. In fact, he was hardly ever near her at all. In that sense she was extremely free and extremely contented. She could concentrate on her job, and even occasionally bring work home.

It was at this time that she confirmed what she had suspected about herself all along: she not only enjoyed the job she was doing, but she actually enjoyed working. She enjoyed working with figures – co-ordinating them, correlating and graphing. She also had more time to give to other aspects of her job. Like not only being able to be present at nearly all the important office meetings, but also sitting attentively through them and fully participating.

Of course all this was different from how things had been in the past. Now she had almost lost the harassed feeling that had attacked her every late afternoon of every working day: that she had to hurry home, or to the market or the shops to buy something, or do something in connection with her role as a mother, a wife and a home-maker. Of course, when she thought of her daughter, she felt a little bad too. But there was no doubt at all that she enjoyed the fact that she was free to attend all the conferences, workshops, seminars and symposia on her schedule, whether they were held inside the country or outside. Then on one of her trips abroad she had met a cousin who did her a great favour. He had helped her buy a small personal computer – for which it was agreed that she would pay the equivalent of its price in local currency to his mother when she arrived home. After she had installed the computer in her house, she virtually worked all the time. It was almost like before she had got married the first time and had had a child.

Esi did not know exactly when the change started taking place in her. Later she began to wonder whether it was the Bamako trip. Perhaps Ali became a little more concrete for her as a being once she had met his father, his 'mother' and the other people from his past. In Bamako, she had also met the other Ali, the French-speaking dutiful son. That Ali was no less or more charming than the one she already knew, but the encounter had completed him for her in a way she could never have foreseen or thought possible. So they had returned south with her almost falling in love with him all over again. Besides, after the introduction to his roots, she felt she had become more of his wife. This inevitably led her to expect him to become more of a husband. If this feeling was not conscious, it definitely was subconscious.

Then there was also this talk of having children. Even if she had been keen on the idea – and God knows she was not – she now wondered how the children were going to be made when she and Ali did not seem to get together often enough to make even one child.

Clearly, the change was due to many things happening or not happening at the same time. For instance, there were many weeks in a row followed by weekends when she did not have to stay at work and do overtime or take work home. She felt at such times that she could do with company without her having to go out and look for it. Of course she had tried at such times to pretend to herself that it was just human company she missed. However, she could also not run away from the fact that Ali was supposed to be her husband, and she missed him. Just as Ogyaanowa was her daughter and she missed her. The comparison worked for her, although she knew they were not exactly the same type of relationship. But from then on, it took her only a short while before she began to wonder about the kind of relationship she had with Ali, and the kind of marriage she was involved in. In fact, the delay in her awakening had been due to the fact that, precisely because they met so seldom, when they did, they got so busy enjoying one another's company that she could hardly remember he had been away so long.

Then something she couldn't find acceptable began to happen. She learnt that Ali had developed a habit of dropping his secretary home at the end of the working day. Esi became even more uncomfortable when she remembered that Ali had acquired a new secretary, a rather pretty and really tiny person with big eyes and unbelievably charming ways. The first time she had gone to Ali's office and seen this new secretary, she had been reminded of a kitten, and she had returned from there feeling quite disturbed. Later that evening, Ali had gone to Esi's, which got her wondering whether he had sensed that something was wrong. One never knew with Ali. That evening it had been on her tongue to ask him why he had not told her that he had got a new secretary. But she

139

had bitten back her words, knowing she would have sounded very foolish. If that girl was the new secretary Ali was dropping home regularly, then Esi realised the signs were bad.

Also from this time, Esi noticed – or was it just her imagination? – that Ali had suddenly developed a marked tiredness and an impatience in his voice any time she phoned him. He would have 'just come back from a trip', and would complain of being 'really worn-out', 'exhausted', 'just a little tired', and did she mind if he phoned . . . or saw her later? At other times, he informed her from the other end of the line that he was 'just this minute leaving the office to catch a plane'. On such occasions, he was 'terribly rushed', he 'simply had to run', and 'darling I shall phone as soon as I land' wherever he was going, or 'back home' or go and see her 'straight from the airport.' It became a pattern. Sometimes he remembered to phone. At other times he didn't. But she never saw him. Not much.

One day around this time, Esi and Opokuya bumped into one another at the market. Esi was wearing a rather pretty *boubou* which combined with her figure for a totally stunning effect. So it could only have been a close and caring friend like Opokuya who could also have noticed that in fact there was something slightly lost in Esi's eyes. Opokuya didn't comment on it though. She just filed it.

Instead, she commented on the *boubou*: how pretty it was, how becoming, and feminine it made her look. Esi was flattered and almost simpered, and she confirmed what Opokuya had guessed: that she had acquired it during the trip to Bamako. But Opokuya was to notice any time they met over the next few months that the slightly lost look never left her friend's eyes.

20

That year's end turned out to be perhaps the most desolate time Esi had spent in all her life. She not only felt tired like everyone else at that time of year, but she was also restless and lonely. She could not plan anything for the coming holidays. This was mainly because she kept hoping that Ali would come to stay for a reasonable length of time: during which they could decide on what they would do together. But in all the six weeks between the end of October and the middle of December, she saw him only twice, and on each occasion he was just breezing through. He would promise that when he returned from wherever he was going the following week he would come to hers, and be properly there. He readily admitted that they had a few things to sort out. But he never came.

By the twenty-third of December, Esi was a nervous wreck. She had only half-heartedly done some Christmas shopping. She had not had the courage even to plan vaguely for any get-togethers at hers to which she would invite friends, or extended family members who lived in the city. She had received a number of invitations though; but she was almost sure that she was not going to go anywhere. Even her attempt to have own daughter with her for the festive season had not only run into snags but eventually ended in a fiasco.

She had gone over to Oko's mother at the beginning of the school holidays to tell her that she would like Ogyaanowa to come to the bungalow for the Christmas and New Year period.

'What ever for?' Oko's mother had asked her.

Esi couldn't believe her ears. Was Ogyaanowa her daughter or not? If she was, why should she need to explain to anybody why she wanted them to be together? Oko's mother had put on her 'dear-God-why-do-I-have-to-suffer-this-witch's-visits?' look, and then proceeded to talk to Esi: very slowly, like the half-wit she took the latter for. Did she remember the last Christmas? Or was it New Year? Why did she want to expose the child to her chaotic and useless life again?

Esi thought she might tell the older woman that the chaos she was alluding to had not been her creation, but her son's. But then, as she had been asking herself over and over again, what was the point? No one in that household ever listened to anything she had to say. They hadn't when she was married to Oko and they were not about to, especially now that she had divorced him. She was aware of a strong temptation to stop going to the house and forget about Ogyaanowa. But apart from the fact that her own mothering instincts revolted at the mere thought, she also knew her mother and grandmother would not let her do that. They had already scolded her for agreeing to let the child go to Oko's people. Besides, she had a secret fear that Oko and his family were working the child against her anyway. She would only make things worse for herself if she cut even her occasional visits to that house. Already, she had noticed that the child never showed any desire to go away with her. Of course Ogyaanowa was always happy to see her; however, Esi thought she had dragged her feet a bit any time she had taken her to go spend the odd weekend at the bungalow.

In the end, Esi had had to agree to do without her daughter's company on the old well-beaten premise that there was no sense in taking a child from a house and neighbourhood full of children to the 'cemetery' that was where she lived.

'After all, Christmas is for children,' Oko's mother had ended the discussion grandly, as if she had just discovered that other festivals were not for children. And all this was why Esi was later to think that the only positive thing she had done that whole year's Christmas period was taking her daughter's present of new clothes and sweets to her.

Meanwhile, she had also toyed with the idea of just packing up on Christmas Eve and going to the village to be with her people. She would return to Accra for the two or three working days between Christmas and the New Year, then return to the village for the New Year weekend, and stay there through the rest of the holidays. But the thought of not having decent answers for the questions she was sure her people would ask her had depressed her so much that she gave up on that idea too. That had not been an easy decision to make though. She kept being sure and not being sure. Half of one day, she was going to the village; the other half she was not. As late as Christmas morning she had packed a few things into her old car and started it. Then a feeling of despair so heavy had overwhelmed her; it was almost like nausea. Of course, she knew her unhappiness was partly caused by her suspicion that her car could break down on the road. For some time now, it had only just managed to take her to the office and back. And since she had not even planned the trip to the village properly, she had not remembered to ask her regular fitter to check on it. Now it was just too late. On Christmas morning, who would be near a workshop even if they were Muslim? In any case, she had not researched the fitter's religion.

She turned off the ignition, rolled up the car's windows, got out and went back into the house. By now she could not believe the mess she was in. She tried to sit and think things through, but she was getting nowhere at all. She finally decided to have a drink, a fairly strong one, and slept the rest of the day through.

By New Year's Eve, Esi had decided that she needed some tranquillisers for her nerves. Like any member of the late-twentieth-century African and other world female élite and neo-élite, she had always known of tranquillisers. At least since she was at the university. After all, you were supposed to become aware from your first year on campus that just about everything in this life ruined nerves:

telephone calls that never came;

cosy weekends that never materialised;

knowing your best friend wanted your boyfriend instead of the one she was going out with;

knowing your best friend's date was so much smarter than the inarticulate somebody who was dating you;

not knowing how to handle male-chauvinist lecturers who didn't even make the effort to read your essays properly because you were a woman;

wanting to be a nuclear physicist but everyone telling you it's much safer to go into teaching because, you know, isn't that too much for a woman? . . . and wouldn't that be too exotic anyway for Africa?

Esi had never taken any tranquillisers because she also belonged to the group around the world who were convinced that taking any such thing was a sign of weakness. But now, as she trudged through the twenty-seventh, twenty-eighth, twenty-ninth and thirtieth of December, she also became convinced that she had coped all she could with the muddle that her life had become. She could not cope any more. So before the second set of holidays caught her, she went to see a doctor friend for a prescription.

The doctor was surprised, since he was no stranger to the belief held in their circles that Esi Sekyi was 'a real tough bird'. But then he too had been practising medicine long enough not to be surprised any more about human beings: their minds or their bodies. To his questions, she answered simply that she couldn't cope with work and her private life. He had got an idea of what had sent even this toughest of birds to him – from the free bag of rumours that circulated around Accra – but he still tried not to probe her for the details. After all, he was not exactly into psychoanalysis. Esi, too, offered nothing. So he gave her a routine and good-natured lecture about the need to guard against addiction, and prescribed her some diazepam.

Having carried the tablets home, Esi realised that she needed courage actually to start taking them. That first night she didn't take any. She went to bed early with a novel which she soon discarded. She tried to listen to the radio and failed. The songs sounded juvenile, and the news gossipy. She could not gather enough energy to play her own music either. Eventually she lay on her back, sweating and wide-eyed. At about three o'clock she drifted off into an uneasy sleep.

The next day was of course the thirty-first and the last day and night of the old year. It was also a Thursday which meant that the first day of the new year which was a holiday would be a Friday. She could see the weekend stretching ahead like the Yendi–Tamale road when it was first constructed: straight, flat and endless.

At about nine in the evening, and absolutely convinced it was a

144

bad omen for the coming year, she took the prescribed milli-grammes. After some initial restlessness she fell asleep.

She slept through the midnight and early morning racket that normally sent off the old year and ushered in the new – the ships' sirens booming in from Tema harbour; the bells of the different Christian churches ringing to the accompaniment of penny crackers cracking; and the earliest of the various tin-drum mendicants already out on the streets, their raucous discords mixing with the singing of serious choral groups. She never heard a thing. She slept through them all: especially since she had bolted her gate the previous afternoon. This meant that even if she had not slept a drugged sleep she would only have heard the singers as the groups paused briefly outside her gate and moved on.

It was a persistent car horn which woke her up. She jumped out of bed and snatched up her housecoat to put it on and rush out. But as the horn blew again it occurred to her that whoever was driving the car had already assumed that she was in, and was therefore going to keep on blowing the horn until she appeared. So she decided that she might as well take a minute to look decent. She felt like stretching. She stretched. Then she rushed to the bathroom, cleaned her mouth, washed her face and looked at it in a mirror. It looked okay but peculiarly puffy. She put on the housecoat and glanced at the clock on the wall in the sitting-room. It read some minutes after seven. She was alarmed. Slept for ten straight hours? This needs thinking about, she thought briefly. Then she was wondering who it could be at the gate as the horn blew yet again. She went to the front door and quickened her pace to get to the gate. The car did not look familiar at all. No, she had never seen it before . . . Then Ali jumped out of it.

Esi screamed, 'Ali!' and was now fully awake – that is, if she had not been before. But then she went straight into another form of stupefaction as she stood staring from one side of the gate, Ali on the other, the key to the gate dangling in her hand.

The car was brand new. It had a maroon exterior and a plush-looking interior. It also appeared quite small and very expensive. As for Ali, there he was, looking so handsome and smiling like a little boy who knew he had done something so fantastic that congratulations from expected quarters were going to take place in some particularly affectionate form. He was not just expecting it. He knew he would get it.

'Ali,' Esi said again and now she herself was not sure whether the exclamation was meant as an acknowledgment of the sight of him or the car or both. Ali climbed back into the driver's seat and asked if he could enter the gate. She woke up from her stupor, opened the gate and stood aside for him and his car to pass. Then she shut the gate again and followed him in. Meanwhile, Ali had already parked by Esi's car. Beside the brand new and rather posh one Ali had just brought, the old car suddenly looked weatherbeaten, shrunken and forlorn. It was almost like a tired human reaction to vigorous unfair competition.

Ali jumped out of the car again and met Esi for a greeting hug. Funnily enough, all the plans she had made over the last several days of how she was going to receive him when – if ever – they met again seemed to have simply vanished. Oh, she was going to be noticeably cold. She was also going to ask him what he wanted at her place, and order him to turn back immediately and leave her premises. The plans were many, but one way or another she was going to get him to see that she was not only fed up but for her, the relationship was finished. But now here she was feeling so relaxed from having slept so well. So that although she knew there was nothing positively wild in how she was feeling about him, there was nothing negatively wild in it either. Definitely, she had no urge to run and scratch his face. Maybe if she had done, or shown her anger in any of the other ways she had planned, Ali would have felt better. As it was, Ali noticed her quiet reserve, and his heart sank.

'Happy New Year, my dear,' he said as he kissed her on the mouth. She did not reject the kiss. When her mouth was free, she said.

'Happy New Year to you too, and what a lovely car!'

'You like it?'

'Of course. Who wouldn't?'

'I am glad,' he sighed with obvious relief. 'Because it's yours.'

'W-h-a-a-t?'

'Of course. Whose did you think it was?'

'But . . . but . . .'

146

'But nothing. This is your car, and here are the keys.'

Esi was aghast. 'How can you give it to me?' she protested.

'Why not? It's your New Year present.'

'But it is too much!'

'Is it? Well, I don't think so.'

Then Esi was touching the car, opening its doors, examining the upholstery, the dashboard, its space-age headlamps. She obviously couldn't believe her eyes or him.

They were both quiet for a little while, and then she faced him fully: 'But what will your wife say?' she asked.

'Please Esi, don't make me angry,' he said it very quietly, and Esi knew he was already angry.

'Well?'

'Well what?'

She had stopped examining the car completely, her eyes on his face.

'I know I've got some explaining to do. But please, let's not fight. It's New Year's Day.'

'It is, isn't it?' Esi countered, as if her surprise that it should be New Year's Day was genuine. She could not understand herself and her lack of excitement. A brand new car? Considering the state her old car was in? Considering that new cars had completely disappeared from the streets of the city? And vanished from the roads of the country? Couldn't she whip up just a little enthusiasm at such an incredible present?

Esi tried, but she could not experience any joy. Surprise, yes. Amazement even. Then she secretly admitted that she had known even before Ali actually said the words – that he had brought the car for her, and she had understood the gesture as a bribe. A very special bribe. But a bribe all the same – like all the other things he had been giving her. They were all meant to be substitutes for his presence.

When she looked up, Ali was watching her. She knew he was reading her mind and she felt a little ashamed.

'Ali, I am so sorry,' she offered as she moved to kiss him. 'Thank you so much . . . It is beautiful . . . And God knows I need a car, a good car . . . This has taken my speech away . . . I don't know what to say . . . I never dreamed I could ever get anything like this . . .'

'I understand,' was all he could say. Then, disentangling himself, he went to open the boot of the car and brought out his briefcase. He opened the case and brought out the papers on the car: licence, insurance, road-worthiness and ownership registration. It was all done.

'You mean that all I've got to do is get in and drive it?' Esi was freshly surprised.

'Exactly,' Ali said. Esi laughed for the first time that New Year morning.

'Hold up your hand,' Ali commanded and Esi instantly remembered the last time he had commanded her to hold up her hand. Slightly puzzled, Esi held her hand up and Ali dropped the keys into her open palm. 'You want to try it out?' he asked her, but Esi thought they should go inside first.

'No, we've been standing here since time began and . . .'

'Actually yes.' Ali agreed, without waiting for her to finish.

'So come in. Let's go sit down and I'll fix us something to eat and drink first.' Esi finished.

They went indoors, and made some toast and a pot of coffee. They ate in silence. The tension had almost gone out of the atmosphere except perhaps for an unspoken understanding that, outside the car, virtually any other conversation topic was potentially explosive.

'How did you know maroon was my favourite colour?'

'Maybe I didn't. I like seeing you in maroon. It's a colour I like too. So I chanced it.'

'Oh Ali, thank you. Thank you so much.'

'If you thank me again, I will probably spank you,' he warned, and they both laughed. It was almost like old times.

But then two mature people cannot talk about a car forever. After they had eaten, Ali told Esi that he had to leave. Esi had suspected this, and deep down she did not even care. But she also felt that at least because of the car, she had to pretend she didn't want him to leave. It was show time.

'Must you?'

'Yes, I wish I could stay . . .'

He couldn't stay. She knew that.

"Could you give me a lift please, madame?" he pleaded playfully.

"Yes, of course!" she agreed, almost too quickly.

She got into the car. She put the key into the ignition and backed out, turned and drove towards the gate. They remembered that he would have to get out to shut the gate. But all that was done in no time. As they faced the open road, Esi looked at him and asked in the even thinner voice of her uncertainties:

'Am I dropping you home?'

'No,' Ali said evenly. 'I'm checking in on one of those visitors at the Twentieth Century.'

'On New Year's Day?' she asked, and then she could have bitten her tongue.

'Yes,' replied Ali.

She could only knead her mouth in despair, as she silently drove them to the Hotel Twentieth Century and parked.

There was neither pain nor joy when she held out her cheek to be kissed. He kissed her and jumped out of the car. She sat for a while watching his disappearing back, as he bounded up the few steps of the hotel, and vanished into its interior.

Esi was flabbergasted. Or rather, 'flabberwhelmed'! Then she laughed softly to herself as she remembered the freakish word. Trust Ghanaians again. They had decided to create out of 'overwhelmed' and 'flabbergasted', a new word to describe an emotional state which they had decided the English were not capable of experiencing, and therefore had had no expression in their language for . . .

Yes, flabberwhelmed. That was what she was feeling as she sat in her excellent new car on New Year's Day at the hotel's car park. Obviously, Ali was determined to keep her off his and Fusena's home. As her heart began to pound rather uncontrollably, she asked herself a question. To wit: in what way was her situation different from what it would have been if she had simply stayed as Ali's mistress, in spite of going to see her people in the village, giving her the ring and all?

The question was out. A shudder ran through her as she began to examine its full implications. And the conclusion came rather swiftly. This was a complete dead end.

The ancients claim that they know something about the freshly dead. That especially those who perish violently are often

149

compelled by certain forces to visit familiar people and places. When they do, they observe what goes on, but without interest. They cannot be moved because all emotions have to do with living tissues: sensitive skin, muscle and bones; rushing blood and beating hearts. And since spirits are humans who have been mercifully spared of such baggage, they cannot rejoice, they cannot hurt . . .

So like a spirit newly released from the body, Esi sat and remembered all the other times in the past that Ali had announced he had to leave her – after a short or a long stay – and how intensely she had hurt each time then.

'I must be running home . . .'

'I have to go home . . .'

'I'll phone from the office before I go home . . .'

'I'll pass by on my way home . . .'

And they had both known that he had always meant where he and his wife, Fusena, and their children lived.

21

Once she was back outside her gate Esi realised that in fact she was not at all keen to enter the house. She turned back towards town. The city was quiet now. The merrymakers of the early hours of the New Year must have dragged their exhausted bodies one by one home to bed. It felt quite strange driving through an Accra that was quiet at mid-morning, and with hardly any traffic. She and her car were cruising as central an area of the city as Makola. Yet even from that far, she could hear the Gulf of Guinea rumbling: like a deep voiced complaint, computerised and programmed to go on forever.

Soon she began to get that special feeling of power that a solid car always gives its driver. She could feel her body and her mind losing the little tension they had managed to accumulate from the last couple of hours with Ali, in spite of the drug and the night's rest. Now she smiled to herself as she thought of what a driving experience this was compared with the struggle her old car had been. She slowed down and began to think. Should she go and show the car to her daughter? She cancelled the idea immediately. Although she was not superstitious, she still couldn't bear the thought of Oko's family looking at her lovely car with their customary malevolence. Should she leave the city centre and take one of the major arteries out? Where would she go? For a moment, she thought of driving home to the village. But knowing how it always was at home, she thought that would be a stupid risk. No one dashed in there and dashed out again. If you arrived there and left six hours later, that would be considered no visit at all. As they saw you off to your car, everyone would be complaining and no one would mind if you heard them. Meanwhile, it was already close to noon. Even if she made up her mind not to go back home to pick up anything but to drive straight on, the trip in would take an hour and a half, at least. If it was still daylight when she left the village, that would be another hour and a half. So that with the unlikely chance of everything working out perfectly one was still looking at about nine hours from then. And it would already be dark anyway when she set out from the village. And she knew the state the roads were in . . . On the other hand, if she was not going to make it a day trip, then she had to go home and pack a few things.

In the meantime, here she was making her way towards Sweet Breezes Hill. Maybe she wanted to go to Opokuya's anyway, to see her and wish her and her family a happy New Year? But, of course, also to show her the car? They hadn't met in a long time, and definitely not once during the holidays. And in any case, it had been like that for some time. Of course, people always made a fuss about leaving newly married people to themselves whenever the circumstances allowed it. Very modern, very educated. Quite untraditional. But apart from that, Esi had suspected for some time that Opokuya was reluctant to come visit her at the bungalow because she really had not managed to deal with 'this second wife business' . . .

Esi nearly turned back when it occurred to her that Opokuya might not be in after all. She always worked on New Year's Eve and other times like that, she remembered. And one thing Esi was quite clear of was that she did not feel like meeting Kubi when Opokuya was away. He had always given her an uncomfortable feeling which she had not tried too hard to analyse. Could it be love/hate? But then why? She had noticed that since she had become Ali's second wife he had been even chillier with her. And that whole trouble the previous year had not helped matters at all. On the other hand Esi felt that if Kubi was just keeping a candle burning for Oko, then it was a bit silly. After all he, Kubi, should know that Oko was a full-grown man who should be capable of taking care of his own problems.

But she continued driving towards the Dakwas'. In a short while she was turning into their drive, and one of the kids had seen her. So by the time she had parked, the whole clan was out there exclaiming. And Opokuya was there after all. Esi got out of the car and the two of them went through their usual exuberant greetings, their questions and answers sliding over one another like eels in a water tank. Then Opokuya was virtually hustling Esi towards the kitchen. Esi caught sight of Kubi as they entered the courtyard, and they waved genially at one another. Of course the friends had lots to talk about, but first the recriminations. Why hadn't this one looked that one up and all that . . . ? Explanations. Excuses. Confessions. As usual, they quickly forgave one another and exchanged New Year greetings. Esi wanted to know how come Opokuya was off duty. What new miracles had occurred? But Opokuya hardly heard her. She was just waiting to hear about the car.

'Esi, and this car . . . Oh it is beautiful . . . It looks completely new. It is, isn't it? Is it yours? When did you get it? . . .'

'One at a time, my sister.' Esi admonished.

'But tell me something quickly,' Opokuya pleaded, as if her very life depended on what Esi told her about the new car.

'It is a New Year's present from Ali.'

'W-h-a-a-a-t?'

'Yes.'

Opokuya opened her mouth. No sound came out. She shut it again. For some time she kept doing that: opening and shutting her mouth. Then it was Esi's turn to be surprised. In all the years of their friendship, she had never ever seen any piece of information or indeed anything at all kick and crush her friend in that way . . . And did she think of 'kick'? And 'crush'? In any case, why should her getting a new car from Ali have that effect on Opokuya, who now stood, a little pathetic, as she opened and shut her mouth like fish out of a drag-net, desperately hopping around for water on a hot beach? It looked a bit funny too.

But how could Esi laugh? Plainly, Opokuya didn't know how to handle the information or all the unexpected and conflicting emotions it had aroused in her. On one hand, she was really happy for Esi. But she was also feeling envious: very envious. And that was quite new to her nature. She was wondering how any one person could be so lucky. And in any case, where was her luck? What was it she had got out of life and out of marriage? Answer: a

153

very faithful husband. Four fine children. Endless drudgery at work. And the state, who was her employer, paying salaries so low you were convinced the aim was to get people like her to resign and go to work for doctors in private practice. Now look at her, and look at Esi . . .

Eventually, Opokuya asked Esi what she planned to do with her old car. Esi told her the truth: that she had not thought about it. 'Sell it to me,' said Opokuya. It was a plea that seemed to have come from so deep in her being, it had almost sounded like a prayer.

Esi was completely taken aback. Sell that useless thing to Opokuya of all people?

'Opoku, it is scrap!'

'Well, sell it to me as scrap.'

Esi looked at her friend as if Opokuya was someone she was meeting for the first time ever.

'Opoku, if you really want that car, you can have it for free,' she surrendered. But Opokuya was not having any of that. Before Esi left Sweet Breezes Hill, they had agreed on a price that was reasonable enough for Opokuya to have the car for next to nothing and still maintain her dignity.

It was late afternoon when Esi finally drove down the hill to return to her place on the other side of town. Clearly, she had not lost any of the dread which had haunted her earlier at the thought of entering her bungalow. Although she had not consciously set out to go and talk to Opokuya, now she was thinking that she should have tried to. How could she have wasted all that opportunity? She felt like whipping herself. Yet she could recall quite clearly how at the time it had seemed as if it was Opokuya who was in need of friendly attention. Besides, how could she have communicated her doubts about the man who had given such a tremendous gift to a friend who had so nakedly envied the gift? Esi was convinced that at some point she had even heard Opokuya murmur that if this was the stuff of which being second wives was made, then her whole life, not just her ideas, needed reviewing! Of course, in her own great way, Opokuya had made it all sound like a joke. Except that over the years it had become quite apparent that it was not only Opokuya who had got to know Esi; Esi too had come to know

Opokuya. And one thing she had come to know about her friend was that all that cheerfulness sometimes carried great anxieties; personal and not so personal. Now Esi was quite certain that some of the personal anxieties had almost surfaced that afternoon. There had been a desperation in Opokuya's voice when they were discussing Esi's old car, which was overwhelming and which Esi would not have believed Opokuya capable of, if she had not heard it herself. But she had heard it: at exactly the point where Opokuya had feared that Esi would not sell her the car precisely because it was old, full of troubles and the sort of thing you did not sell to your worst enemy or a good friend – because an enemy would take it that you knowingly cheated, and a good friend would feel deliberately betrayed. No, you sold cars like that either to total strangers you were never likely to meet again, ever, in your life, or to Kokompe engineers for cannibalisation. To think Opokuya was the one who would drive the car made Esi feel very, very uncomfortable . . .

Well, the least she could do would be to hand the car over to her favourite 'engineers' even before she had taken a *pesewa* from Opoku. They would work thoroughly on it; reorganising it completely with spare parts manufactured by themselves. It might take about six months, but that would cut the total cost by about two thirds. And she knew that when they said they had finished, it would have the possibility of at least another year's trouble-free driving to it. These were proposals the mechanics had made to her a long time ago. But she had not been able to take advantage of it because she could not see how she could have done without the car for that long . . .

Esi continued sitting in the new car outside her own gate while the night built itself up around her. She was having arguments with Ali, with Opokuya and her own self – about Ali, about the two cars and above all about Ali's new secretary.

So what of it if Ali occasionally dropped his secretary home?
But it was not 'occasional'. It sounded like every day.
So what of that?
But I don't want him to!
Why not?
It hurts.

Does it?

Terribly!

Well, just remember that if a man can have two wives . . .

Then he can have three wives . . . four wives . . .

And on and on and on . . . Plus, remember . . .

Esi did not want to remember anything. She got out of the car, opened the gate, entered the compound and parked it for the night. Soon she was getting ready for bed, composing her thoughts for another working week and for a brand new year.

22

Things did not improve. In the first few weeks of the
new year, it could be seen that Ali was trying. He made his visits to
Esi's more regular, and stayed as long as he could, whenever he was
around. It was almost like before they got married. But he really
could not keep it up. Too soon, things returned to the pattern of the
very recent past.

Ali phoned regularly to announce his imminent departures. He
phoned from the different cities and towns inside and outside the
country to which he travelled. He phoned to report his arrivals. In
between his travels, he phoned regularly when the telephone lines
permitted. He and Esi always had good telephone conversations.

He also sent gifts. And what gifts! He brought her gold bangles
from the Gulf States and succulent dates from Algeria (or was it
Tunisia?). He brought her huge slabs of chocolates from Switzer-
land, and gleaming copper things from Zambia and Zimbabwe. He
brought her shimmering silk from the People's Republic of China,
the Koreas and Thailand. Indeed, he virtually made a collector of
the world's textiles out of Esi as her wardrobe literally overflowed
with different types and colours. From West Africa itself she got
gorgeous *adires* from Nigeria, as well as other fabrics from Mali,
Sierra Leone and the Gambia. These were all various shades of blue
extracted from the wild indigo plant and either put on comfortably
coarse traditional weave, or on imported fabrics of programmed
softness and perfected sheen. From the Soviet Union, Ali brought
Esi some very special amber-inlaid wrought iron jewellery as well
as the cutest *matroshkas* for Ogyaanowa. Then, since he seemed to
have made it a policy to bother with only Japanese electronics, he
brought her from other technologically advanced environments,

their ethnic goods and local crafts. Or if they were manufactured goods, then they would be peculiar to the place and unrivalled anywhere else in the world: household linen and native American jewellery from the United States, beer mugs from Bavaria. Through the gifts, Esi saw the entire world from her little bungalow. What she did not seem to see much of was the skin of the man behind the phone calls and the gifts.

The explosion occurred somewhere towards the end of their third year of marriage. Esi decided she was just fed up. For weeks she had not seen Ali. So one day when the gate had been open and she had heard a car drive up, she peeped at it through the curtains. It was early afternoon of a weekday and she had just come in from work herself. She was only dressed in a single piece of wrapper. When she realised it was Ali, she didn't bother to go and change. She just met him at the front door with, 'Ali, I can't go on like this.'

With one hand clutching some parcels and his briefcase, he tried to grab her for an embrace with the other hand, even before he had entered the sitting room completely. But Esi would not let him. And since he was carrying too many things and one hand was completely occupied, she could easily wriggle free.

'I said I can't go on like this,' she repeated. Ali seemed to have heard her this time. He dumped everything in a nearby chair and moved towards her. But Esi quickly moved back and kept walking backwards and away from him like a child who had done wrong and earned a whipping. Or rather, as if Ali carried some dangerous contamination and had to be kept as far off as possible. Ali noticed it all and stopped in his tracks, hurt.

'Esi, you say you can't go on like what?'

'Like . . . this,' she said shrugging her bare shoulders. Almost as if her condition of being scantily dressed and barefooted early on a tropical evening was a symbol of the condition of their marriage, and therefore his fault. 'This is no marriage.'

'What would you consider to be a marriage?' He asked, his voice full of genuine puzzlement.

'I don't know,' she replied. And she was being genuine too. 'But if this is it, then I'm not having any of it,' she added with such chilling finality that for a little while, Ali really did not know what to say. Then he turned, went back to the chair and picked up only his briefcase and turned to leave.

'If that's how you see it, then I'm going –'

'Home!' Esi finished the sentence for him with something of a flourish, like a victory declaration. 'Well, just go "home" to your wife and children and leave me alone,' she told him, more quietly.

Ali was clearly confused. For a moment or two he shuffled on the same spot; then he opened the front door and went out. He must have gone straight into his car and turned on the ignition. Soon Esi heard the car move away. She collapsed into a chair, her eyes shining while a headache began to work its way up from the back of her neck.

About three months later, Esi phoned Opokuya at the hospital. Opokuya noticed immediately that her friend's voice sounded extremely tired. This was a new Esi she was teaching herself to get used to. The first time Esi told Opokuya about the break up, she could hardly speak for the suppressed tears and sniffling. Opokuya had already learned that Esi and Ali were through, that the marriage was 'comot, kaput, finished, kabisa.' Opokuya had not been at all surprised. But she had pretended that she was. If you don't tell such truths easily to yourself, then how can you tell them to your best friend? So calling up her composure and good sense, she told Esi that she was terribly shocked by the news.

'Are you sure of what you are telling me?' she breathed into the phone. 'What has happened? . . . When did it happen?'

Meanwhile, Esi was laughing hysterically.

'Opokuya my sister, just tell me that you told me so!' she screamed.

Opokuya could only do the best a phone would permit. She begged Esi not to distress herself. Because everything would work out in the end. At this, Esi laughed harder. Eventually, Opokuya promised to go over and see her at the next available opportunity. Esi seemed to be immediately comforted by that. She calmed down and even managed to remember to tell Opokuya that the next time she was at the bungalow, she could drive the car away, because in the course of the year she had got it repaired and repainted, and now it was looking really good. Opokuya was so excited at the news that waiting through the next few days was pure torture.

Opokuya wanted to come that evening or the next, but something always cropped up at home or at work. So that whenever she was really free, it was always too late and too dark. But today she was determined to see Esi and to take away the car, even if she got there at midnight. She had been on a morning shift, but whoever should have come to relieve her in the afternoon had been so late that she had virtually done the afternoon too. Of course, she had told herself that she was not going to mind. That apart from depriving her of a good break, it suited her fine. When the night shift came, she would go straight to Esi's.

But things turned out even better for her. The afternoon person came eventually, very late for work, but quite early for Opokuya's plans. So she arrived at Esi's at virtually the same time as Esi had herself just got home from work.

They went indoors together and had a little chat. Esi made tea for Opokuya and fixed a drink for herself. Or a series of quick drinks. When Opokuya commented on it, Esi flared up asking her what was wrong with one having a drink or two after work. Opokuya was finding it all distressing. But there was nothing she could do to help her friend. She secretly wished Esi would weep or do whatever else would get some of the tension out. But she also knew that her friend was not the weeping kind.

Eventually, Esi gave the car keys to Opokuya, who was so thrilled that she nearly flew out of the door. But then something occurred to her and she looked sharply at Esi.

'But Esi . . . eh . . . don't you need your old car yourself? I mean isn't Ali . . . taking the new one back?'

Esi understood. 'No, it's all right. Ali says the car is mine . . . So you just go and enjoy your car!'

Opokuya released a huge sigh of relief.

The evening ended up being one of the vary rare times the friends had been together, and yet after a while they did not seem to have much to talk about. This was due to the fact that Esi was still feeling low over her problems with Ali, and Opokuya was too excited at the immediate prospect of having her own car. Which meant that Esi wanted to be alone, and Opokuya was in a hurry to be gone. Finally, Opokuya managed to leave Esi, and get into the car. She drove away. It was dusk, but too early to switch on the car's headlamps. In any case, for all the clarity of her vision and the confidence of her steering, Opokuya could have been driving on the motorway at high noon.

Esi stood in the space left by her old car and listened to its engine as it wheezed away. She forgot that it was quite late, and she should go and lock the gate. Instead, she turned and went indoors. She shut the front door behind her and made straight for her bedroom and her bed. She sat down. Then to her own surprise, she started to weep. Nothing violent: just two tears rolling quietly down her cheeks.

23

All Esi was aware of was desolation. As for her mind, it was completely blank. She did not know what to do and was not sure whether she had to do anything. What made everything bad was that she had been aware that her grandmother and Opokuya had tried very hard to warn her. She had just been a real fool. What was she to do? Where did she go from here? Too tired to do anything else, she continued to sit on the edge of her bed while the tears too continued streaming down her face. After a while, she thought she should get up, go and wash her face and begin to pull herself together. But even that seemed like such a massive operation; as though someone had tasked her to rebuild the world. She continued to sit.

She probably dozed for about half an hour with the sheer exhaustion of everything. Because when she looked out the window, she couldn't see anything at all. Night had fallen without her being aware of it. She realised that she was sitting in the dark, and her bedroom was not the only place without lights. There were no lights anywhere in or around the house. She also remembered that she had not shut the gate or locked any of the doors. She told herself that, much as she hated the thought, she should just get up and get ready for the night.

Then she saw the lights of a car. She had not heard it come in, and wondered who it could be. She got up and started putting lights on; a little action she was to regret, because if she had just stayed where she was, the caller could have concluded that she was not in and gone away. But once she had put the first lights on, she had to continue, and there there was no chance of her pretending that she was not in.

So who could it be? There was of course Ali . . . but it couldn't be him. It could be Opokuya who might have been coming back for any one of a number of things to do with the car . . . The visitor was already knocking on the door as she switched on the light in the sitting room. Perhaps she should switch on the light on the veranda for whoever it was; but she felt that she may just as well open the door and let the person come in anyway. As the visitor stepped into the room, she shut the door and stepped back.

Neither of them could collect himself or herself together quickly enough even to say hello. They just stared. Kubi was overcome by the sight of an Esi he had not seen before; eyes of crimson and face stained with tears. And Esi was feeling extremely vulnerable since she suspected that that was how her face looked.

'I thought Opokuya was here,' he said rather uncertainly.

'Yes, she was here but she's gone now.'

'How?'

'In my car,' she said, and tears welled up in her eyes.

'What is it?' Kubi sounded alarmed. Esi lifted her face to say something to him . . . No words came. Kubi took hold of her hand, maybe to lead her into the room and get her to sit down. He found himself holding her close. Then, as though he had taken a quick decision just in that minute, he turned to face her and hold her closer and hard. She did not feel like offering any resistance. He began to kiss her face, her neck and all over. Then they were moving towards the couch and Esi could feel Kubi's manhood rising.

Esi's mind snapped open. There must be a cure for most pains including a feeling of desolation, she was thinking. Why not? she added, all in her head. Then it occurred to her that maybe this was what had always been between her and Kubi. Which neither of them had wanted to face but which had inspired his treatment of her to swing between that of a kindly understanding uncle and an irritable, disapproving older brother? It also occurred to her that maybe this might be an answer to the great question of how to get one's physical needs met, and still manage to avoid all attachment and pain.

So then, why was she remembering that business about drowning people experiencing a replay of their entire life in a flash of a second? So here was her life. Either it is not true that only the drowning go through that experience, or we can drown quite a few times in this life in different ways . . . And water is not the only force to fear . . .

Thoughts chased one another so quickly in her mind, it was like a fast-moving film . . . She remembered that there is something called friendship. And hadn't her friendship with Opokuya been, so far, the most constant thing in her life? And that whereas mothers, fathers, grandmothers and other relations are like extra limbs we grow, a friend symbolises a choice? And to maintain a friendship is a choice? Therefore not to maintain a friendship – indeed, to kill a friend – is a choice? Opokuya's ample face came into view, beaming . . . humorous, but with Nana's voice, 'My lady Silk, remember that a man always gains in stature any way he chooses to associate with a woman – including adultery . . . But, in her association with a man, a woman is always in danger of being diminished . . .' In any case, wasn't the need to maintain that friendship greater on her part? Maybe Opokuya could shed her. She, Esi, could not afford to shed Opokuya.

When she finally realised that Kubi was unzipping his trousers, Esi broke free from the embrace. And at that sign of unwillingness on her part, Kubi too paused. He might have offered an explanation, but there really was no need for words. He reorganised himself and made sure he had got his keys. At the door Kubi turned to face Esi. It was as if he was going to say something. Again there was no need. Esi easily guessed what he had been about to say. She was never going to breathe a word of what had nearly happened – to Opokuya or any living soul. There are things you don't do to a friend. Opokuya was not just a friend. She was a sister, almost her other self. And definitely there are some tales you don't tell even to yourself.

Esi never went back to Oko. As far as she was concerned, that was never even an option. She never had a baby with Ali either. That relationship stopped being a marriage. They became just good friends who found it convenient once in a while to fall into bed and make love.

She never bothered to look for an annulment of the marriage.

164

That would have meant going back home to her people with her version of what had happened. They would have called Ali. Ali would have shown due respect and gone to meet them at the village. They would have put before him the matter as they would have received it, and expected Ali to comment. She knew that Ali would have told her people that as far as he was concerned he loved her and that they were still man and wife . . . Her people would not have accepted any explanation from her as to why she would want to 'destroy' that marriage too.

'What? Throw away a man who gave you things any other woman would have given part of her life for? Including a brand new beautiful car? And isn't it being rumoured that in fact, he has almost finished paying for an estate house for you?'

'And he is fine!'

'Ah, for a scholar, so respectful . . . an unusual human being . . .'

It would probably have ended in her grandmother asking her to go back to the village for a longer stay. So that they could take her to the priestess and ask her to have Esi's soul called up for an interview. For instance, about what it was that she really desired from this life. Since as far as they were concerned she always seemed to get and throw away what other souls desired. Besides, her behaviour was becoming too unnatural altogether.

No, she could not go through all that. Not really.

So the marriage stayed, but radically changed. All questions and their answers disappeared. If Ali went to Esi's and she was not in, he tried not to question her about it when they next met. For Esi though, things hadn't worked out so simply. She had had to teach herself not to expect him at all. She had had to teach herself not to wonder where he was when he was not with her. And that had been the hardest of the lessons to learn. For, Accra being that kind of place, she couldn't help hearing about his womanising activities. Given the nature of her job, it was only natural that out of those close to Esi, it should have been Opokuya who heard more of the gossip about Ali. Yet it was she who told Esi least. Esi believed Ali when he insisted that he loved her very much. She knew it was true: that he loved her in his own fashion. What she became certain of was that his fashion of loving had proved quite inadequate for her.

So what fashion of loving was she ever going to consider adequate? She comforted herself that maybe her bone–blood–flesh self, not her unseen soul, would get answers to some of the big questions she was asking of life. Yes, maybe, 'one day, one day' as the Highlife singer had sung on an unusually warm and not-so-dark night . . .

Glossary

zongo
West African term for a ghetto of northern peoples in southern cities. Most people who live in zongos are presumed to be Islamic.

tuo
A Hausa staple adopted by almost the entire Sub-Sahel. It is made from rice, millet, corn or sorghum.

kola
In current West African pidgin, this means a bribe.

ninos
A Ghanaian expression for a new recruit, interchangeable with 'greenhorn'.

harmattan
The cold, dry wind that effectively constitutes the West African winter.

armstrong
Tightfisted. West African pidgin pun on the Scottish name.

The Castle
Christiansburg Castle by the sea at Osu, Accra. Built by the Danes, it was subsequently captured by the English who used it as the seat of colonial government. Except by President Kwame Nkrumah, who ignored it for symbolic reasons, it has been preferred as the residence and offices of all governments.

kenkey
A coastal Ghanaian staple of cooked corn meal and one of the solid foundations of a vast national food industry.

nim
A tree common in coastal Ghana. It produces sweet, edible berries.

dokon-na-kyenam	dokon: real name for kenkey, *see above*
	kyenam: fried fish.
	Always put together as a standard fast meal, eaten cold.
wahala	Pidgin, meaning troubles or disagreements.
abe nkwan	Soup prepared from the fruits of the palm nut tree.
kolof rice	Classical West African meal of rice with stewed meat and vegetables.
Makola	The centre of Accra where there used to be a huge two-part market.
Kokompe engineers	Dealers who sell used-car parts and have their market in Kokompe, which is a large area north-west of Accra.
pesewa	Smallest unit of Ghanaian currency.
adires	Traditional Yoruba batik.

Afterword

by Tuzyline Jita Allan

I

Once in a while I catch myself wondering whether I would
have found the courage to write if I had not started to write
when I was too young to know what was good for me.

Ama Ata Aidoo, "To Be a Woman"

Before reading from her new novel, *Changes*, at the Festival
of African Writing sponsored by Brown University in November 1991,
Ama Ata Aidoo recalled the early stages of her career. Her subject
matter, she jokingly reminisced, had provoked a peculiar style of
greeting from an influential African male literary critic. "How is my
little girl with Africa and women on her shoulders?" he would inquire
in half-jest.[1] The remark drew muted laughter from her rapt Ivy League
audience on whom both its paternalistic tone and allusive intent were
clearly not lost.

The greeting's combined sense of levity and seriousness captures the
gap between African women's literary enterprise and the critical
establishment's response to it. Aidoo and other African women artists
bear the prodigious responsibility of holding in check the structures of
gender and cultural domination. Yet this feat remains curiously unac-
knowledged by an African critical paternity that has managed to
propel the African imagination onto the world stage and many male
writers along with it.[2]

In "To Be a Woman," an essay that qualifies easily as a manifesto of
African feminism, Aidoo links female subordination with the
marginalization of the woman writer in Africa. Women's victimization, she points out, begins with the distinction made at birth between
"a girl [and] a human being," the latter category designating the male
child (263). She believes that this demarcation underlies the masculin-
ization of the public sphere and the attendant exclusion of women

from it. She recounts her own experience as a writer and an academic with male colleagues who resented her independent spirit and tried to portray her successful first novel, *Our Sister Killjoy Or Reflections From a Black-Eyed Squint* (1977) as unAfrican. Aidoo is both saddened and offended by this act, calling it a "violence" intended to insure the death of the female author (262).

Of course, critical immolation of the woman writer is not unique to Africa. The long list of casualties compiled in the West by feminist critics during the past two decades attests ruefully to the universality of the epistemic violence inflicted on the female artist. For African women, however, this fact is compounded by the presence of a literary nationalism bent on purging the creative (female) mind of such corrupting Western influences as feminism. At a recent African writers' conference, the Ugandan writer Taban lo Liyong presented the definitive nationalist argument against feminism:

> I suspect that feminism may destroy that which up to now has enabled Africa to withstand all the buffeting from other cultures . . . I think I should appeal to keep the African household intact at the end of the day, otherwise we may have our younger sisters going off and joining in dances in Lapland which concern the people of Lapland only. (*Criticism and Ideology* 183)

Responding, Aidoo correctly identified this nationalistic plea for cultural purity as a ploy to silence women:

> To try to remind ourselves and our brothers and lovers and husbands and colleagues that we also exist should not be taken as something foreign, as something bad. African women struggling both on behalf of themselves and on behalf of the wider community is very much a part of our heritage. It is not new and I really refuse to be told I am learning feminism from abroad. . . . (*Criticism and Ideology* 183)

Aidoo's retort foregrounds the unexamined assumptions that African femininity is inherently nonfeminist and that the (borrowed) elements of Western feminism exhibited in African women's writing are inimical to African nationalism. Both assumptions have no basis in fact, but together they have proved effective as a strategy of alienation. Internationally, images of African women's passivity and easy accommodation to society, rooted in colonial discourse, underlie mainstream Anglo-American feminism's indifference to the African female subject. And while some women critics in England and America have begun to focus attention on African women's writing, the Western opinion that feminism is alien to African women seems unshakable.[3]

This act of dismissal abroad stands in ironic contrast to the fears expressed at home about African feminist practice. The nationalist grounds on which these fears rest diminish, however, once one understands African women's literary purpose. Women writers in Africa feel as deeply as their male counterparts the need to repair Africa's fractured image following colonialism. But they also intend to interrogate cultural prerogatives that circumscribe women's lives. In short, they interpose gender in the pivotal project of African cultural recovery. Theirs is a bold and decisive gesture of synthesis aimed at dissolving the false dichotomy, implicit in nationalist discourse, between female and national liberation. Adeola James, in a recent interview with the Kenyan female writer and educator Micere Githae Mugo, put the matter this way: "Will it damage the ultimate struggle for a complete social, economic and political liberation of Africa if we focus on singing the song about the oppression of women?" (98)

Aidoo's own artistic response to this question represents a forceful argument against the view that divides woman and nation. "One must resist," she writes, "any attempts at being persuaded to think that the woman question has to be superseded by the struggle against any local exploitative system, the nationalist struggle or the struggle against imperialism and global monopoly capital" ("To Be a Woman" 264). As the bit of ironic confessional release in the epigraph to this essay indicates, the author's courage of conviction on this matter has proved costly, especially in African literary criticism where attitudes toward her work run the gamut from neglect to outright hostility.[4] Yet her belief in the necessary, albeit uneasy, connection between woman and nation remains unshaken. If her work focuses on the points of rupture between these two entities, it is to underscore the need for their reconciliation. Put simply, Aidoo believes that post-independence Africa cannot afford to ignore women if it wants to succeed in nation rebuilding. She sums up both her artistic vision and her aesthetics in a recent article in *Dissent*:

When people ask me rather bluntly every now and then whether I am a feminist, I not only answer yes, but I go on to insist that every woman and every man should be a feminist—especially if they believe that Africans should take charge of our land, its wealth, our lives, and the burden of our own development. *Because it is not possible to advocate independence for our continent without also believing that African women must have the best that the environment can offer.* For some of us, this is the crucial element of our feminism. (323, emphasis added)

II

I feel the revolutionalizing of our continent hinges on the woman question.

Ama Ata Aidoo, in Adeola James, *In Their Own Voices*

The publication of *The Dilemma of a Ghost* (1965) warned us to expect painful truths from Aidoo even as it opened her formidable career. The play is a remarkable harbinger of her favorite themes: the fractured modern African psyche, the chasm between Africa's past and present and the difficult but necessary search for links, the torment visited on Africans by European colonization, and the indomitable African female spirit. Another major imprint left by the play is the Aidoo-esque tone. It is at once doubting and hopeful, scathingly ironic and deeply longing, a paradoxical combination of resistance and identification that makes Aidoo one of the most ardent voices in a troubled postcolonial age. This dialectic, however, embodies more than the spirit of anxiety that rules the modern African soul. It is a call for action, for an effort of will to resolve the painful dilemma of African life in a world of change.

The Dilemma of a Ghost prefigures the important role women play in this effort. The play's crisis centers around the cross-cultural marriage of two young college graduates: Ato Yawson, a Ghanaian studying in the United States, and Eulalie Rush, a young African American woman. Ato's confident return home with his wife provokes a classic confrontation between past and present, between tradition and modernity. His marriage puts him on a collision course with his family on several fronts: his wife is a cultural outsider (a "black-white woman"), a descendant of slaves, and the holder of strange views about motherhood. Caught between the competing demands of his wife and his family—and, by implication, the West and Africa—Ato feels as torn and devitalized as the folkloric ghost immortalized in the children's song appropriately titled "The Ghost." Like that "wretched" figure of childhood imagining (28), his response to crisis is not action but paralysis.

Ato's dilemma is an epistemological one. He must reconcile two opposing systems of knowledge in order to maintain a coherent sense of self. His failure, in Aidoo's mind, bespeaks more than personal ineptitude. It exemplifies the disorientation and sense of irrelevance that afflict his class, namely, Africa's intellectual bourgeoisie, described in *Our Sister Killjoy* as "comatose intellectuals" (121). Esi Kom's intervention is important because it is she who recognizes the epistemological nature of her son's problem and its attendant irony:

> *But do you never know anything? I thought those who go to school know everything* . . . so your wife says we have no understanding and we are uncivilised . . . We thank her, we thank you too . . . *But it would have been well if you knew why she said this.* (50, emphasis added)

Esi Kom's reprimand is directed mainly at her son's failure of imagination in the face of conflicting systems of thought. The pull from both sides has left him powerless and, not coincidentally, speechless, a fact that his face-saving retreat into rigid masculinity (he slaps Eulalie) cannot conceal. His mother's scolding, therefore, also carries with it the implicit message of the need to create alternative thought systems that operate outside the crippling economy of power. This valuable epistemological insight is summed up in Trinh Minh-ha's pronouncement: "Between knowledge and power, there is room for knowledge-without-power" (40). Esi Kom's resolution of her son's crisis through acceptance of his "black-white" wife clears the ground for the construction of such a power-free knowledge system.

The picture Aidoo draws in her first published work of the oppressive and unimaginative nature of existing structures of knowledge is developed in her second play, *Anowa* (1970). The setting here is nineteenth-century colonial Ghana, to which the writer turns in part to challenge long-standing myths about African womanhood. The most stubborn of these myths—that African femininity is congenitally passive—is debunked by the heroine's spontaneous and ample spirit of rebellion. Anowa does not embody the feminine ideal of the "good woman [who] does not have a brain or mouth" (93). On the contrary, she is equipped both verbally and intellectually to do battle with her parents, husband, and community over the legitimacy of her own ideas.

For Aidoo, the marriage plot, with its penchant for constraint and conformity, seems an appropriate site to test the strength of her heroine's ideas. Anowa violates several marriage conventions: she refuses to marry early, rejects socially approved suitors, and chooses her own mate. The marriage plot is further radicalized by the feminization of Anowa's husband-to-be. The most watery "of all watery males" (75), Kofi Ato is a diluted male, a female-man, the incarnation of a masculine culture's nightmare.

This subversive beginning, however, gives way to an aggressive reassertion of the marriage plot with Kofi Ato's self-transformation into a greedy, power-hungry egomaniac intent on fulfilling his capitalist dream on the backs of slaves. Anowa feels betrayed but neither her outrage nor her refusal to accede to her husband's lust for power can avert the outcome of the marriage plot: the heroine's death as punishment for her rebellion. Anowa's suicide measures her entrapment within patriarchal law. Her search for freedom thwarted, she chooses death as the means of escape for her dissident spirit.

While Aidoo chooses to work with the the marriage plot in *Anowa*, she leaves behind sufficient reason to hope that if and when it resurfaces in her later work it will undergo a careful reappraisal. If, as the play's legendary origins stipulate, Anowa's tragedy is a cautionary tale for would-be violators of marriage's patriarchal law, it also serves to put Aidoo on notice about the need to rechart its course to allow women, in Margaret Atwood's words, "to go somewhere else" other than the grave.[5] The choral voice of wisdom that ends the play makes it clear that change is both desirable and inevitable: "Who knows if Anowa would have been a better woman, a better person if we had not been what we are?" (124) In *Changes* Aidoo explores this question to determine the extent to which African women and their nation have come of age, but it is first given apocalyptic urgency in the multi-genre arena of *Our Sister Killjoy*.

The simmering problem of intellectual dislocation dramatized in *The Dilemma of a Ghost* comes to a boil in *Our Sister Killjoy* with the brazen acts of accommodation by "academic pseudo-intellectual[s]" (6), educated Africans seduced and beguiled by Western cultural hegemony. Sissie, the protagonist, is a new invention: the African woman as artist-heroine, measuring in a punishingly ironic tone vast levels of social and moral decay in "twentieth-century modernia" (22). The despoilers of this landscape come from the frontlines of the political and intellectual arenas of Europe and Africa. The novel's

176

emotional logic, however, is guided by the desire to dislodge the bourgeois mentality that feeds a host of social problems in contemporary Africa—from obsequious politicians who feel a kinship more with De Gaulle and Edward Heath than with their constituents, to intellectual aspirants, like Sammy, for whom "going to Europe was altogether more like a dress rehearsal for a journey to paradise" (9). For Sissie, the bourgeois mind is pseudo-intellectual, a veritable symptom of a failed imagination. It engenders, for example, such obdurate naiveté as revealed in Kunle's reading of a biracial heart transplant in South Africa as marking the end of racialism.

Equally disturbing is pseudo-intellectual indifference to the woman question. In the "love letter" that ends the novel Sissie links Western cultural and African male hegemonies in an effort to compel a rethinking of African "group survival" (114) that includes women. She contests her double silencing—as an African, forced to "use a language that enslaved me" (112) and as a woman, socially conditioned to "shut up and meekly look up to [the male]" (117). She calls for a new idea of nationhood, one that reconceives women as subjects, pseudo-intellectual thinking as a threat to national well-being, and Africa's common folk—the formally uneducated mothers and fathers of formally educated Africans—as part of those "intangible realities" that make for "life being relevantly lived" (129).

Sissie's epistolary conflation of the personal and the political provides an insight into Aidoo's own textual practice. Writing against the common understanding that proscribes women's experience as tangential to national life, she has gone as far as renegotiating the relationship in revolutionary terms. A mother's timely intervention in her son's politically-charged crisis (*The Dilemma of a Ghost*), Anowa's holy rage against patriarchal inexorability, Sissie's politicization of a personal adventure—these narrative acts of resistance are all framed by the desire to break down the border separating women and the state. Aidoo's interest in the dissolution of boundaries derives from a unique understanding of the changing African environment. Like many African writers weaned on *Things Fall Apart*, she realizes that change is the inevitable outcome of the colonial experience. Also, like some, she is ambivalent about change, recognizing its potential for both good and harm. What Aidoo brings to the subject, however, apart from a keen geopolitical sensibility, is a heightened awareness of the complex nature of change. Necessary, slow, insidious, liberating—these are but a few descriptions of the faces of change in her work.

177

Aidoo's commitment to female autonomy, her belief in a salvational force preserved in pockets of traditional African life, and her knowledge of the destructive nature of oppression combine to create a fervent and conflicted voice for change that speaks with compelling authority in *Changes*.

III

I cannot see myself as a writer, writing about lovers in Accra because you see, there are so many other problems.

Ama Ata Aidoo, *African Writers Talking*

Readers familiar with Aidoo's oeuvre will agree that *Changes*, winner of the 1992 Commonwealth Prize for Literature in Africa, is a novel she was bound to write, in spite of doubts she expressed twenty-five years earlier about her capacity to write a love story amid the turbulent climate of post-independence Africa. Such readers may at first be amused by the prefatory "apology" and "confession," which refer to the writing of the novel as "an exercise in words-eating," but, on second thought, will fit these tropes into the ironic mode so typical of the author's expressive manner. For the fact is that the love plot is a common feature in Aidoo's work, although it is embedded so seamlessly into weightier concerns that it often escapes the attention of critics who pan solely for political gold. For example, the relationships between Eulalie and Ato, Anowa and Kofi, and Sissie and her unnamed lover in *Our Sister Killjoy* are generally subordinated to the "loftier" issues of cultural conflict, communal authority, and cultural disintegration, respectively. Such a critical practice unfortunately ignores Aidoo's habit of coupling the personal and political.

Put in proper perspective, Aidoo's statement, used here as an epigraph, reflects artistic intent or practice less than the political and gender realities of the time. In 1967, in the midst of a nationalistically-charged political climate filled with post-colonial possibility, Aidoo—one of only a handful of women writing in Africa[6]—could not afford to convey the impression of neglecting the big "problems" of the day to frolic in the private chambers of love. Admitting a proclivity to the personal (read: women's experience) was a risk the woman writer knew well enough not to take. Hence, although Aidoo at the time of the interview had written two plays and a few short stories in which private and public domains are fused, it seemed more prudent to accentuate the latter in an interview.

Placing *Changes* in the thematic continuum outlined above is not to deny or underplay its innovative character. The novel pulses with an irrepressible pioneering spirit, clearing the ground for a new tradition of women's writing in Africa. It is a record of the changing circumstances of women's lives in contemporary Africa, but more importantly it transcends realistic significance and constructs a psychological blueprint for female portraiture. Based on the novel's cumulative impact, African women's diminishment in literature may well be a thing of the past. The three main female characters together provide a composite portrait of an emerging African femininity from which many future experiments will be drawn. Educated, career-oriented, financially independent, and strong-willed, Esi Sekyi, Opokuya Dakwa, and Fusena Kondey are also wives, mothers, and daughters, a combination that replaces the ideal of domesticity that has long governed the imaging of women in African literature. It is not a utopian vision, however. Obstacles to the full humanity of women threaten even the most promise-filled female act. In other words, *Changes* is as much about stasis as it is about change. Yet the novel enlarges women in ways hitherto unimagined by the producers of African literary culture.

Aidoo returns to the institution of marriage, the seat of patriarchal power, for signs of the changing relations between women and men, and the results are mixed. On the one hand, a bad marriage is no longer inherently tragic for women. The loud communal tones of censure that drove Anowa to her death have died down to a family whisper of disapproval with Esi's termination of her marriage to Oko. Esi's financial independence is not an unrelated factor. Her path-breaking career—she is a statistician with a master's degree—earns her more money than her teaching husband and, following their separation, an African literary record is made: the husband must vacate the family home because it belongs to his wife. One need only recall Anowa's dispossession and placelessness to fully appreciate Esi's achievement. For Opokuya and Fusena, too, financial stability proves a protective advantage, although the latter's circumstances, the most comfortable of the three, are enhanced not by the career she had planned to have but rather by a compensatory gift from her entrepreneurial husband who scuttled that career.

Women and money not only make for imaginative capital, as Virginia Woolf accurately noted,[7] but also for a transformative psy-

179

chological economy of marriage. In *Changes* the major women characters resist victimization mainly because theirs is a habit of mind unaccustomed to the consolidation of power in male hands. Esi, for example, rejects Oko's plea for sympathy for the daily bruising to which he claims his ego is subjected because of his wife's atypical femininity. In retaliation, and to assure himself that in spite of her culturally aberrant behavior, "Esi too [is] an African woman" (8), Oko rapes her. Esi's response to her violation occurs in three quick stages. First, she names the act: it is "marital rape" (11), although there is no "indigenous word or phrase for it" (12) in her linguistic universe. Naming the rape act enables Esi to read it not as an oxymoron, as masculine logic would have her believe, but rather as a patriarchal tool designed to enforce female subjugation. This reading is reinforced by the post-rape narrative moment that shows Oko walking away from Esi's naked body, dragging the "sleeping cloth" behind him, "look[ing] like some arrogant king" (10). The scene evokes antithetical images of subject and object, exaltation and humility, power and powerlessness, and Esi knows on which side of the gender divide she falls. But she also knows that the divide is a social construction designed to limit, even deny, her humanity. From this knowledge springs action, a forceful reassertion of the self, that culminates in her separation and divorce from Oko. Esi's refusal to participate in the post-rape ritual of victimization is an integral part of the novel's effort to reconstitute female identity.

Acts of self-legitimization by Opokuya and Fusena also require significant expenditure of emotional capital, and they too have the backing of stable incomes. Opokuya's comes from a fifteen-year career as a registered nurse and midwife, and Fusena's business is rumored to have "made more money . . . than the largest supermarket in town" (67). Oko's representation of Opokuya as "a good woman" typifies male misreading of female signature. His search for a "proper" model of femaleness to negotiate Esi's self-desocialization inhibits his understanding of Opokuya's complex personality. This complexity is masked, for instance, by her obsessive concern for Kubi's physical well-being. The self-serving motives underlying Opokuya's maternal attitudes should not be overlooked. One is simply a matter of survival. With four children and a family not within close proximity, her self-interest seems to overlap significantly with genuine concern.

The maternal mask also allows Opokuya to deflect deep anxieties about her husband's (in)fidelity. An extension of her nursing instinct, Opokuya's "worry" about her husband's safety enables her to continue to "work" at home and thereby remove herself emotionally from her husband who, as the final scene shows, is actually as untrustworthy as she suspects. Work proves to be more than an emotional palliative for Opokuya. It is also a conduit for financial independence, a fact she asserts forcefully with her purchase of Esi's car to ease the strain of daily rounds between work and home. Old and well-worn, the car clearly does not measure up to required transportation standards (Ali describes it in the opening scene as dangerously "frail" [4]), but it serves as a fitting symbol of the old and oft-forgotten fact of African women's industry and financial autonomy

Unlike Opokuya and Esi (before the latter marries Ali), Fusena has no car worries. Her "two-door vehicle" may look inconsequential beside her husband's "elegant and capacious chariot" (99), but it makes for easy travel between her "kiosk" and home. Her problems begin when her worst fears come true. Earlier on, Fusena had abandoned her plans for an advanced degree and a teaching career, married her college friend, Ali Kondey, and settled into a wifely and childbearing routine that took her to England and back home to Ghana. As she watched Ali fulfill his dreams through several degrees, she began to fear that the educational gap opening up between them would eventually engulf her. The incarnation of this self-fulfilling prophecy is Esi, the elegant, well-educated divorcée Ali chooses to be his second wife. Fusena's response to her husband's remarriage plans seems to complicate the novel's paradigm of a changing (African) female personality within the marriage plot. Lacking voice, she is unable to articulate even her anger. In fact, Fusena's entire range of self-expression is comprised of eight brief statements, four of which are one-to-five-word interrogatives. But judging from her reaction—the dangerously reckless manner in which she drives out of the house to go to work on the day she gets the news—her rage is tremendous. It definitely belies the image of the woman whose first and last words in the novel represent nodding approval of patriarchal authority—"yes" to Ali's marriage proposal and a triple "yes" to the women summoned by "the patriarchs of Nima" (105) to console her. Fusena's silence, therefore, bespeaks not the absence of an inner life but rather her double isolation within the dominant society and, in particular, her own restrictive Muslim culture. She appears silent because she is "not being heard."[8]

The tensions embodied in the portrayal of Fusena and Opokuya—not to mention Esi in her role as Ali's second wife—reflect the novel's dual themes of social stasis and change. Echoes of the former reverberate throughout the novel and frequently appear in ironic juxtaposition with the latter. The opening chapter's conflicting images of womanhood set this pattern in motion. We see, on the one hand, a highly educated female employee of the Ghanaian government making travel plans to attend an international conference with her male colleagues and we observe, on the other, the gendered dynamics of a social environment that threaten to weaken her leverage. This conjunction of female capability and vulnerability, captured at the end of the chapter by Ali's categorization of Esi as both "fascinating" and "frail" (4), is dramatized in the rest of the novel through the separate and interlocking lives of the three women characters.

New attitudes about marriage also appear against an immovable background of cultural beliefs and practices. Esi's sense of independence, for example, stands in opposition to the view of woman as object of exchange embodied in the "breathing parcel" (71) Oko receives from his mother as replacement for the ungovernable Esi. A man of fiercely traditional instincts, Oko sees his career-driven wife as part of a disturbing modern trend, but even he is shocked to learn that "it was still possible in this day and age to get a young woman . . . who would agree to be carried off as a wife to a man she had never met" (71). Ali, too, is rudely awakened to the facts of custom when he shows up before Esi's "fathers" with one of his employees to ask for their daughter's hand in marriage:

> "You take someone who by age, kinship, social standing or wealth is in position to stand firm in all matters to do with the well-being of [the] marriage. Above all, he or she must be one who in a crisis must be respected and deferred to by all parties concerned. Your own employee? No-no." (103)

Not to be outdone, Ali's father explodes in anger at his son for failing to consult with him and other "real" family members before marrying a non-Muslim woman. The anger is short-lived, but it demonstrates tradition's show of force in the face of encroaching change. Ali himself is an amalgam of the competing claims of Africa's old and new realities. A French- and British-educated, well-traveled business executive, he remains firmly grounded in the patriarchal view of woman as "occupied territory" (91). His preference for sexually-ripened women does stand at one remove from his father's forays into virginity, but his purchase in the economy of sexual pleasure is as large. Ali's feminine looks—a "smooth . . . black" skin, "beautifully even and white" teeth, and "kohl"-darkened eyes (22)—combine with a new age charm to produce an irresistible and punishing lure. Negotiating polygamy turns out to be more arduous than he had imagined and his bouts of guilt over Fusena's hurt feelings betray a modern sensibility. But for Ali, these are ultimately petty cares next to the thrill of victory over the female body. Esi's is a new site of voyeuristic pleasure, an experience he complains of being hitherto deprived by "a great number of women" (75), including Fusena. Magnificently compensated by Esi's unabashed sexuality, Ali uses the patriarchal privilege of polygamy to claim exclusive rights to yet another sexual terrain.

The novel's innovative force, however, resides in how Esi mediates the contradictory impulses of tradition and modernity that influence the outcome of her "love story." Some readers will likely rally around the opinion that Esi's embrace of polygamy wrecks the liberated self she projects at the beginning of the novel. Her hasty re-entry into a sexual relationship after the rape, which was intended to control her, may cause additional wariness about her feminist capability. Such views, however, would fail to consider an important narrative detail: Esi's consuming desire for a self-fulfilling career. The collision between female career goals and monogamy becomes all too apparent to Esi in her first marriage. Oko's smothering need to be mothered undermines her effort to compete in a work environment where she is outnumbered and demeaned by men. In full retreat from monogamy's compulsory domesticity, Esi takes a second husband whose primary care belongs to his first wife, leaving her with ample time to pursue what she euphemistically refers to as "my lifestyle" (48).

If Esi's grasp on her freedom slackens under Ali's gaze, the cause lies less with her will than with the nature of romance. The romantic peril is its penchant for controlling women and Esi, love-struck for the first time (she had felt only gratitude for Oko), is an ideal target. The novel offers a parable of the incompatibility of female autonomy and romance. As Esi gets entangled in love, her sturdy independence begins to turn flabby, leaving her enervated almost to the point of a nervous breakdown. Caught in a quandary of dual loyalty—to her career and to Ali—she gives an ironic nod to her previous marriage, in which the battle lines were more clearly drawn. The novel resolves the dialectic by deftly evoking the specter of erotic control to alert women to its danger. When Esi finally awakens from its hypnotic power, she performs two important acts of self-recovery. The first is her rereading of Ali's lavish gifts not as tokens of affection but as bribes aimed at weakening her resistance. The second is her rejection of Kubi's near-rape act at the end of the novel, a move that posits heterosexuality as a threat to female bonding. The novel's culminating stance thus offers female friendship as a site of resistance against the erotics of control. Breaking the silence on erotica in the African novel, Aidoo at once locates it within patriarchal ideology and explodes it. Taking its place is a reservoir of good will between two women—Esi and Opokuya— that stretches through their multiple roles as wives, mothers, and career women. Theirs is the novel's preferred model of love, a strong, nonoppressive current of feeling that flows between two women.[9] Both Ali's spasms of affection and Oko's domineering passion fail the test.

Acts of self-authorization in the novel are not restricted to modern women. Nana, the embodiment of traditional womanhood, intervenes at a crucial point in the plot through a subversive rendition of the myth of male supremacy that opens the way for her grand-daughter's emotional recovery. Esi's consultation visit with her "mothers" to seek approval for her marriage to Ali presents the older woman with the opportunity to tell her version of the gender story. The result is a double-voiced narrative that both affirms and subverts the military metaphor of woman as "occupied territory." On the surface, Nana's account of male occupation of the female body seems approving. Conventional images of divinity invest the invasive act with the grandeur of griot-narrated legend. Close inspection of this female griot's story, however, reveals a satirical edge undercutting the grand-stand image of maleness. The following sentences illustrate her narrative method:

Who is a good man if not the one who eats his wife completely, and pushes her down with a good gulp of alcohol? (109)

Men were the first gods in the universe, and they were devouring gods. (110)

Under Nana's skillful control of language, seduction and violence combine to imprint the male psyche. The same paradox characterizes romantic love, marking it as a strategy of male dominance. She drives

184

home the point in a memorable pronouncement: "a man always gained in stature through any way he chose to associate with a woman" (109).[10] This statement, the centerpiece of her cautionary tale, is both a warning and prophecy. Unheeded, it exacts from Esi a heavy emotional price. That it embeds in her mind, however, is evident in her decision to break with Ali and to reject Kubi.

It is to Nana, then, that we, like Esi, turn to unravel the novel's intertwining chords of change and stasis. While she joins the chorus of women's voices that laments male intransigence in a world of change, she also believes strongly in women's self-emancipating ability. Her narrative articulates a sustainable strategy of resistance: the systematic dismantling of men's allegorical claim to power. To unseat the idea that, in her words, "some humans [are] gods and others [are]sacrificial animals" (111) is her call to arms. And, by linking the economies of male and colonial domination (she refers to "equally implacable" and "bloody" European gods [110]), Nana reaches the critical threshold in Aidoo's work where gender and nation meet. Not surprisingly, her prescription for progress—an interplay between "a lot of thinking and a great deal of doing" (111)—involves Aidoo's twin strategies of female and cultural recovery.

In *Changes*, Nana's countermyth of male supremacy and Esi's difficult but successful negotiation of romance testify to the possibility inherent in female "thinking" and "doing." The thought/action dyad is present throughout Aidoo's writing. It explains the sense of female agency that gives her work its distinctive character within the tradition of women's writing in Africa. Aidoo's creative imagination has no room for the drama of victimization believed to preoccupy African women writers. Missing from her work is the painstaking delineation of women's oppression by such writers as Buchi Emecheta and Flora Nwapa (modern Africa's first published woman novelist). Female disadvantage in Emecheta's fiction, for example, is ubiquitous and deterministic. The process of women's subjugation is often over-whelming, and escape from the prison house of gender is virtually impossible. Nnu Ego, the most valiant of Emecheta's heroine-victims, captures this pervasive sense of female frustration in an existential plea: "God, when will you create a woman who will be fulfilled in herself, a full human being, not anybody's appendage?"(*The Joys of Motherhood* 186)

One would be hard-pressed to locate the idea of a besieged feminin-ity in Aidoo's work. Even the somber mood of *No Sweetness Here* (1962) allows for female agency. Women in these stories are mothers, wives, sisters, aunts, grandmothers, and subjects. The title story, which predates *The Dilemma of a Ghost*, depicts a woman, Maami Ama, in the throes of a divorce from her brutal husband. She stands to lose her only child, a handsome ten-year-old boy, to her husband if he wins the case. The alternative, however, petrifies her spirit even more. Maami Ama's self-affirming decision is captured in a question that sharply contrasts with Nnu Ego's: "Why should I make myself unhappy about a man for whom I ceased to exist a long time ago?"(62) The happiness accompanying her freedom is shortened by the tragic death of her son, but there is every reason to believe that she will survive that too.

Indeed, as *Changes* vividly demonstrates, the cult of motherhood has no fanatical following among Aidoo's female characters—another of the author's distinctive characteristics. Far from lacking the maternal instinct, the women in the novel nonetheless show no signs of yielding to its culturally-enforced power. Esi, for example, is an absentee mother by dint of an active career and personal life. It is her husband, Oko, who, atypically, bears the emotional burden of looking after their daughter's well-being. Opokuya is closer to the idea of hearth and home than Esi, but she too steers shy of maternal guilt. Of particular significance is the lax bond between Esi and her mother, a fact she correctly attributes to the changing face of the mother in contemporary Africa. That "[s]he could never be as close to her mother as her mother was to her grandmother" (114) is a truth confirmed by Esi's own maternal impulse. In Aidoo's short story "Nowhere Cool," the pro-tagonist, Sissie, is also aware of the conflict between the time-honored idea that "mother is gold and mother is silk" (63) and the exigencies of contemporary life. She has left her children at home in Ghana for a three-year study stint abroad and, airborne, she feels small pangs of anxiety. But this feeling is quickly replaced by the compelling fact that to "go she . . . knew she must, pushed by so many forces whose sources she could not fathom" (63).

The emblems of change, locatable throughout Aidoo's work, come together in *Changes* to reveal the turbulent cross-currents of contemporary African life. Ironically, Aidoo confesses that she intended to write a "simple love story," one she hoped would relax the readerly tension of *Our Sister Killjoy*.[11] Whether *Changes*, whose genesis is a radio play written in Zimbabwe in 1988, takes the sting out of Aidoo's first novel will be a subject of heated debate. What is certain is that it is a sobering book. It charts a new mode of cultural consciousness and that is no small undertaking.

IV

They had always told me I wrote like a man.

"To Be a Woman"

Aidoo has said that she is "happiest of all with drama," followed in descending order by poetry and fiction (*In Their Own Voices* 22). What she knows but is too modest to admit is the ease with which she moves between boundaries of genre. In the true spirit of both the oral tradition and modernism, Aidoo abhors the separation of genres and has elected instead to build bridges between literary forms. The resulting mixture of the pithy and the poetic, of fragmentation and coherence, of words that refuse to pacify, has provoked the criticism that she writes "like a man." The rebuff is not new. Women writers in the West have been similarly stung, triggering efforts, as varied as Virginia Woolf's delineation of a woman's sentence to French feminists' celebration of *l'écriture feminine*, to fashion a female style. In Africa, where writing is still considered an exclusively male activity, it is not surprising that a stylistically innovative writer like Aidoo should be tagged a pretender.

There is no pretense, however, regarding Aidoo's commitment to creating new modes of expression to capture the multifaceted character of African life, including its present state of dislocation. For this task she draws from the techniques of both African oral art and twentieth-century modernism. Typically, her narrative method consists of broken thought sequences, dizzying time shifts, elliptical syntax, spare prose, and interior monologues. Amply illustrated in her short fiction, this style explodes in *Our Sister Killjoy*, a fractured and sardonic portrait of modern life. The clash of genres, styles, tones, and rhythms in the work has rendered it unclassifiable. Characterized by critics as novel, prose poem, and novella, and as "fiction in four episodes" by Aidoo herself, the text is a testimonial to Aidoo's unique creative grammar.

A love story, *Changes* is stylistically more relaxed, but Aidoo's fondness for the generic hybrid is just as strong. Poetry, drama, the short story, and the novel form work together to produce linked meanings. Poetic and dramatic divagations, for example, are spaces filled with bits of satire and cultural history that illuminate and reinforce the plot. It is the method of the storyteller, an attempt to engage, entertain, and inform her audience. The following dramatic insert comes after the critical information about the death of Ali's mother after childbirth:

"Was she not fifteen when Ali was born?"
"That was all she was."
"Then how could she have lived?"
"She could not live. She did not live. I saw it all. She looked at the baby Ali very well. You could have thought she just wanted to be sure that everything was fine with him."
"Then what happened?"
"Ah, my sister, may Allah preserve us. She sat quietly and bled to death." (22–23)

This imagined dialogue between narrator and audience creates a heightened sense of tragedy and, consequently, helps to sharpen the criticism of Musa Musa's exploitation of young women. The divagated dialogue between Esi's mother and grandmother over their daughter's ill-fated plan to marry Ali also carries narrative urgency, as these opening lines illustrate:

Ena: What shall we tell the child?
Nana: You have already made a mistake.
Ena: What mistake?
Nana: By calling her a child.
Ena: And isn't she my daughter?
Nana: That she is.
Ena: So then, what crime do I commit if—?
Nana: Please, select your words very carefully. Your daughter—my grand-daughter—has thrown a problem at us. That is what we are talking about. Committing crimes should not even be mentioned here. (112)

Sometimes the divagation provides straightforward cultural commentary. The emotional logic of pre-marital consultations, for example, is reaffirmed in the following definition of parentage to underscore the gravity of Ali's failure to consult with his extended family before marrying Esi. Parents "in the old days" were—and, by implication, still are—

"the father who helped your mother to conceive you, the mother who gave birth to you, and all those who *claimed* to be brothers and sisters to those two" (133, emphasis added).

Foremost among Aidoo's stylistic techniques is the use of dialogue to develop character and plot. At the beginning of the novel's denouement in Part III, for example, dialogue both telescopes time and events and sheds light on Ali's postnuptial persona following his and Esi's honeymoon visit with his Bamako kin. The passage records Ali's telephone performance as he tries to justify his absence from his newly wedded and anxious wife:

> "Okay, if you can wait for a couple of minutes I could drop you home.
> "Hello, yes . . . hello, yes, yes, yes, it's Ali . . . Hi . . . yes. Oh, but I have missed you! Fine, fine. And how are you?
> "Yes, oh yes. About four o'clock this afternoon.
> "Yes, fine.
> "Okay. But exhausting as usual . . .
> "Yes, this time, properly worn out . . .
> "Eh . . . eh . . . I . . . well . . . eh . . . actually I am going straight home to wash out all this travel dirt . . . and . . . nothing at all. Just jump into bed to try and recover from my jet-lag . . .
> "Esi, please try to understand . . .
> "Darling, it's not like you to be unreasonable . . .
> "Not today.
> "Because it's never possible for me to breeze through your place for five minutes . . . please?
> "Yes, tomorrow evening.
> "Oh, definitely, I shall come straight from work. So how about cooking me one of your specialities?
> "Ya . . . Ya . . . Ya . . . Ya . . .
> " . . . Good . . .
> " . . . Lovely . . .
> " . . . See you then. Okay . . . Bye!" (137)

Ali's staccato voice contains tell-tale signs of waning interest, the prelude to what is to become the couple's long distance marriage.

While the poetic and dramatic inserts are legitimate oral devices, the embedded short tale takes a greater resonance within the conventional topoi of African oral art. As digression, it accords both storyteller and audience a necessary break from the narrative, and particularly for the former, a place to rest and recharge. Moreover, when the embedded tale is a throwback to an earlier time, as in *Changes*, it feeds the audience's appetite for the unfamiliar. Musa Musa's crime and self-punishment constitute the novel's tale-within-a-tale. Depicted is a social order so stern that a shepherd boy is forced to flee his home for losing one goat from the herd in his care. Thus, along with its entertainment value, the episode compels comparison with the relatively laxer social context inscribed in the main narrative.

Similes, proverbs, and Africanisms are an integral part of the linguistic identity of Aidoo's writing. They are effective rhetorical tools that capture the communicative rhythms of African (in particular, Ghanaian) life. Take, for example, the simile describing Opokuya's surprise upon seeing Esi's flashy new car:

> In any case, why should her getting a new car from Ali have that effect on Opokuya, who now stood, a little pathetic, as she opened and shut her mouth like fish out of a drag-net, desperately hopping around for water on a hot beach? (153)

Opokuya's visceral response is captured here by more than the conventional fish-out-of-water metaphor. Her shock is measured by an image familiar in West Africa's fishing culture: the stunned reaction of freshly-caught fish emptied from the nets onto hot stretches of sand.

In the following epic simile, the spirit world, a common feature of the African imagination, is evoked to paint a haunting picture of Esi's lovelorn state:

> The ancients claim that they know something about the freshly dead. That especially those who perish violently are often compelled by certain forces to visit familiar people and places. When they do, they observe what goes on, but without interest. They cannot be moved because all emotions have to do with living tissue: sensitive skin, muscle and bones; rushing blood and beating hearts. And since spirits are humans who have been mercifully spared such baggage, they cannot rejoice, they cannot hurt . . . (149–150)

Aidoo's use of proverbs is instinctive and innovative. Proverbs are not ordinarily associated with an urban setting, nor with women, but the few, well-placed ones Aidoo chooses for this story capture the bite and flavor of one of the distinct elements of African literary expression. For Aidoo the African proverb, apart from its verbal dexterity, is a form of social psychology shaped, by persons she endearingly refers to as "ancients," to enhance the collective wisdom. One of Esi's bouts with loneliness, for example, is registered through a cautionary proverb: "having to love a burdensome child because one day you will miss her" (79).

Africanisms, new words coined from the alchemic blending of English and the African cultural scene, enrich Aidoo's linguistic repertoire. Such terms as "flabberwhelmed," "negatively eventful" and "away matches" violate standard English in order to express a socio-linguistic identity that is uniquely African.

Changes' redeployment of stylistic traits common in Aidoo's writing does not lessen its inaugural significance. The novel will both haunt and guide subsequent thinking about women in Africa.

V

> It was from my father I first heard the rather famous quotation from Dr. Kwegyir Aggrey: "If you educate a man, you educate an individual. If you educate a woman, you educate a nation."
>
> "To Be a Woman"

Of the elements that have shaped Aidoo's creative mind, her family is perhaps the most important. Hers is a lineage of political and pro-woman activism that spans a century. Her paternal grandfather was "tortured to death in a colonial prison for being 'an insolent African'"; and her father "supported Kwame Nkrumah . . . and believed that above all, a nation should educate its women."[12] Described as "in her way . . . politicized," Aidoo's mother, Abasemah (alias Elizabeth Bosu), has been a source of nurturing political energy, starting with her "talking" stories that continue to inspire her daughter's art and including her keen sense of national and global politics.[13] But perhaps the best indication of the family's heterodoxy is to be found in a bit of advice the young Aidoo received from an aunt, who, she says, was unschooled in English: "My child, get as far as you can into this education. Go until you yourself know you are tired. As for marriage, it is something a woman picks up along the way" ("To Be a Woman" 259).

Into this family, distinguished by its ability, in Aidoo's words, "to see alternative lives for children other than the one adults were living" ("To Be a Woman" 259), Ama Ata Aidoo (christened Christina) was born on March 23, 1940. Her twin brother was stillborn, one of five of her mother's children who did not survive. A "mercurial, electric, and fearless character," her father, Yaw Fama (alias Manu IV), was *ohene*[14] of the village, a kingmaker of Abeadzi state, which meant that he had a political voice in who became *omanhene*[15] of the region."[16] His, also, was the most persistent voice in ensuring that young Aidoo receive a formal education, in spite of the prevailing bias against schooling for girls.

She attended the Wesley Girls' High School at Cape Coast, the oldest and one of the most prestigious secondary schools in Ghana. It is here that her artistic interest and talent began to develop. Her teacher, Barbara Bowman, now living in retirement in Yorkshire, England, "was instrumental with respect to [her] early awareness of [herself] as a writer."[17] In response to Bowman's question about her students' future goals, Aidoo expressed a desire to become a poet. "Oh but Christina," Bowman replied, "that's good, but you must remember that poetry doesn't feed anybody."[18] A couple of years later, however, Aidoo received a gift of great significance from Bowman: an heirloom Olivetti typewriter. Aidoo's dream would soon be realized, first in fiction, followed by drama and poetry. Her first published work, a short story titled "To Us a Child Is Born," won a Christmas story competition organized by *The Daily Graphic* in 1958. On the strength of her second short story, "No Sweetness Here," Aidoo was invited to the historic African Writers' Workshop held at the University of Ibadan in 1962. It was her first year in college and meeting and making common cause with such literary luminaries as Langston Hughes, Chinua Achebe, Ezekiel Mphahlele, Wole Soyinka, and Christopher Okigbo left an indelible mark on her budding creative mind. That same year she wrote the first draft of *The Dilemma of a Ghost*, whose production in 1964 at the University of Ghana, Legon, and subsequent publication in 1965 secured her place on Africa's emergent, male-dominated literary scene.

The admission of Chinua Achebe's *Things Fall Apart* (1958) into the "Oxbridge" canon at Legon gave Aidoo's artistic confidence a significant boost.[19] "[W]hen I read *Things Fall Apart* I said, 'Oh, so? He can do this,' "[20] that is, retrieve and re-affirm African cultural identity. The novel's genuine attempt to reconstruct Africa's battered colonial image provided a potent stimulus as Aidoo began to contemplate the contours of her own fictional landscape. The anti-feminist attitudes of British professors at Legon may also have helped to sharpen Aidoo's artistic resolve. In English courses, for example, her essays were frequently defaced by outright misogynist comments, such as "Excellent but for feminine carelessness" or "Superior work except for female shoddiness." Small wonder, then, that women constitute a major force in her work. Interrogating male mythologies of female subjectivity is one of Aidoo's well-defined artistic goals.

Commitment to social change has engendered in Aidoo a tremendous versatility. Adding to an array of literary credentials—poet, dramatist, novelist, and essayist—are her roles as university professor, politician, and mother. In 1968 and 1969 she taught simultaneously in the School of Drama at the University of Dar es Salaam, Tanzania, and in the English Department of the University of Kenya in Nairobi. Her tenure as Coordinator of the African Literature Program at Cape Coast lasted for ten years (1972 to 1982). During 1974 and 1975, she served as a consulting professor in the Ethnic Studies Program at Xavier University in New Orleans. Other academic posts include Fulbright Scholar-in-Residence to the Great Lakes Colleges Association in 1988 and Writer-in-Residence at the University of Richmond, Virginia, in 1989.

From 1972 to 1979, Aidoo held directorships at the Ghana Broadcasting Corporation, the Arts Council of Ghana, and the Medical and Dental Council. This period of social activism culminated in her appointment as Minister of Education in 1982. A year later, she left her post and, after a brief visit to France, went to live in Zimbabwe as a full-time writer. The goal of uninterrupted creativity, however, proved difficult. While *Changes* and the radio play from which it originates were written in Zimbabwe, her creative work has had to compete with other commitments, such as teaching and working with the Zimbabwean Women's Writers' Union, the Ministry of Education, and women's tie-dye groups. Thus Aidoo remains steeped in African cultural life, which she, in turn, weaves into a rich tapestry of art.

"[My] daughter, Kinna, has also influenced my writing," Aidoo admits to an interviewer.[21] A graduate of Smith College where she majored in Chemistry, Kinna Likimani was born in 1969 to Aidoo and Ernest Parsali Likimani, a noted Kenyan biochemist, who died in 1980. Kinna's effect on her mother's art extends far beyond the series of poems dedicated to her in *Someone Talking to Sometime*. A vision of the world she will inherit, if gender and cultural domination go unchecked, drives Aidoo's creative imagination. "I have no right to pessimism. There are powerful forces undermining progress in Africa. But one must never underestimate the power of the people to bring about change."[22] Nor can we afford to underestimate Aidoo's own power as an agent of change.[23]

Notes

1. See "Routine Drugs I" in *Someone Talking to Sometime*, p. 61. Professor Eldred Durosimi Jones, to whom the poem is dedicated, made the remark.

2. Sandra Gilbert and Susan Gubar refer to the "literary paternity" of Anglo-American literature. See *The Madwoman in the Attic: The Woman Writer and the Nineteenth-Century Literary Imagination* (New Haven: Yale University Press, 1979), p. 9.

3. Recent critical texts on African women's writing include *Ngambika: Studies of Women in African Literature*, edited by Carol Boyce-Davies and Ann Adams Graves (Trenton, N.J.: Africa World Press, 1986); *Journeys Through the French African Novel*, by Mildred Mortimer (London: Heinemann, 1990); *Motherlands: Black Women's Writing from Africa, the Caribbean and South Asia*, edited by Susheila Nasta (New Brunswick, N.J.: Rutgers University Press, 1992); *Moorings and Metaphors: Figures of Culture and Gender in Black Women's Literature*, by Karla C. Holloway (New Brunswick, N.J.: Rutgers University Press, 1992); and *Binding Cultures: Black Women Writers in Africa and the Diaspora*, by Gay Wilentz (Bloomington: Indiana University Press, 1992). For the view that regards feminism as antithetical to African femininity, see Katherine Frank's "Feminist Criticism and the African Novel" in *African Literature Today* 14 (1984).

4. See Aidoo's essay, "To Be an African Woman Writer—An Overview and a Detail."

5. Quoted in *Changing the Story: Feminist Fiction and the Tradition*, by Gayle Greene (Bloomington: Indiana University Press, 1991), p. 13.

6. Other women writers of this period include Efua Sutherland (Ghana), Flora Nwapa (Nigeria), Grace Ogot (Kenya), Bessie Head (South Africa), Assia Djebar (Algeria), and Rebecca Njau (Kenya).

7. See *A Room of One's Own* (New York: Harcourt Brace Jovanovich, 1929), pp. 37–38.

8. The quotation is Jane Gallop's. See "Snatches of Conversation" in *Women and Language in Literature and Society*, edited by Sally McConnell-Ginet, et al. (New York: Praeger, 1980), p. 274.

9. For another examination of female friendship in African women's writing, see *So Long a Letter* by Mariama Bâ (London: Heinemann, 1989).

10. Virginia Woolf's mirror metaphor conjures up a similar idea. See *A Room of One's Own*, p. 35.

11. February 5, 1993 interview with me in Clinton, New York.

12. See the frontispiece to *Someone Talking to Sometime*.

13. See James, *In Their Own Voices*, pp. 13 and 19. In the February interview Aido cited as an example of her mother's keen political mind her concern over American supply of corn to the military government that overthrew Kwame Nkrumah.

14. An equivalent for this Akan word is "chief," which Aidoo puts in the same category of negative colonial terms as "tribe."

15. Paramount chief is the English equivalent.

16. February 5, 1993 interview.

17. February 5, 1993 interview.

18. February 5, 1993 interview.

19. "Oxbridge" is a conflation of Oxford and Cambridge. Colleges and universities in England's former colonies remained loyal to the English curriculum. See *Decolonising the Mind: The Politics of Language in African Literature*, Ngũgĩ wa Thiong'o (London: Heinemann, 1986).

20. See *African Writers Talking*, edited by Cosmo Pieterese and Dennis Duerden (New York: Africana Publishing, 1972), p. 26.

21. See *In Their Own Voices*, p. 19.

22. February 5, 1993 interview.

23. *The Art of Ama Ata Aidoo*, by Vincent O. Odamtten, the first complete study of Aidoo's works, will be published in December 1993 by The University of Florida Press, Gainesville.

Works Cited

Aidoo, Ama Ata. *The Dilemma of a Ghost and Naowa*. Harlow, England: Longman, 1965.

_____ . *No Sweetness Here*. Harlow, England: Longman, 1970.

_____ . *Our Sister Killjoy Or Reflections from a Black-Eyed Squint*. London: NOK Publishers, 1979.

_____ . *Someone Talking to Sometime*. Harare, Zimbabwe: The College Press, 1985.

_____ . "To Be a Woman." *Sisterhood Is Global*, ed. Robin Morgan. New York: Anchor Doubleday, 1985, 258–65.

_____ . "To Be an African Woman Writer—An Overview and a Detail." *Criticism and Ideology*, ed. Kirsten Holst Petersen. Uppsala,

Sweden: Scandinavian Institute of African Studies, 1988, 155–72.

_____ . "Nowhere Cool." *Callaloo* 13, no. 1 (1990): 62–70.

_____ . "The African Woman Today." *Dissent* 39 (1992): 319–25.

_____ . *Changes: A Love Story.* London: The Women's Press, 1991.

Emecheta, Buchi. *The Joys of Motherhood.* New York: George Braziller, 1979.

Gilbert, Sandra M. and Susan Gubar. *The Madwoman in the Attic: The Woman Writer and the Nineteenth-Century Literary Imagination.* New Haven and London: Yale University Press, 1979.

James, Adeola. *In Their Own Voices: African Women Writers Talk.* London: Heinemann, 1990.

McConnell-Ginet, Sally, et al., eds. *Women and Language in Literature and Society.* New York: Praeger, 1980.

Minh-ha, Trinh T. *Woman, Native, Other: Writing Postcoloniality and Feminism.* Bloomington: Indiana University Press, 1989.

Odamtten, Vincent O. *The Art of Ama Ata Aidoo.* Gainesville: The University of Florida Press, forthcoming.

Petersen, Kirsten Holst, ed. *Criticism and Ideology.* Uppsala, Sweden: Scandinavian Institute of African Studies, 1988.

Pieterse, Cosmo, and Dennis Duerden. *African Writers Talking.* New York: Africana Publishing, 1972.

Woolf, Virginia. *A Room of One's Own.* New York: Harcourt Brace Jovanovich, 1929.

MEMOIR AND AUTOBIOGRAPHY
from the Feminist Press at the City University of New York

Across Boundaries: The Journey of a South African Woman Leader by Mamphela Ramphele. $14.95 paper, $19.95 cloth.

Always from Somewhere Else: A Memoir of My Chilean Jewish Father by Marjorie Agosín. $11.95 paper. $18.95 cloth.

Among the White Moon Faces: An Asian-American Memoir of Homelands by Shirley Geok-lin Lim. $12.95 paper, $22.95 cloth.

Black and White Sat Down Together: Reminiscences of an NAACP Founder by Mary White Ovington. $10.95 paper, $19.95 cloth.

Cast Me Out If You Will: Stories and Memoir by Lalithambika Antherjanam. $11.95 paper, $28.00 cloth.

Changing Lives: Life Stories of Asian Pioneers in Women's Studies edited by the Committee on Women's Studies in Asia. $10.95 paper, $29.95 cloth.

Come Out the Wilderness: Memoir of a Black Woman Artist by Estella Conwill Májozo. $14.95 paper, $21.95 cloth.

A Cross and a Star: Memoirs of a Jewish Girl in Chile by Marjorie Agosín. $13.95 paper.

A Day at a Time: The Diary Literature of American Women Writers from 1764 to the Present edited by Marjo Culley. $16.95 paper.

Fault Lines by Meena Alexander. $16.95 paper.

Juggling: A Memoir of Work, Family, and Feminism by Jane S. Gould. $17.95 paper, $37.00 cloth.

Life Prints: A Memoir of Healing and Discovery by Mary Grimley Mason. $14.95 paper, $19.95 cloth.

A Lifetime of Labor: The Autobiography of Alice H. Cook. $15.95 paper, $29.95 cloth.

Lion Woman's Legacy: An Armenian-American Memoir by Arlene Voski Avakian. $14.95 paper, $35.00 cloth.

The Little Locksmith by Katharine Butler Hathaway. $14.95 paper, $35.00 cloth.

Magda's Daughter: A Hidden Child's Journey Home by Evi Blaikie. $16.95 paper.

Memories: My Life As an International Leader in Health, Suffrage, and Peace by Aletta H. Jacobs. $18.95 paper. $45.00 cloth.

These Modern Women: Autobiographical Essays from the Twenties edited by Elaine Showalter. $8.95 paper.

I Dwell in Possibility by Toni McNaron. $15.95 paper.

Songs My Mother Taught Me: Stories, Plays, and Memoir by Wakako Yamauchi. $14.95 paper, $35.00 cloth.

The Seasons: Death and Transfiguration by Jo Sinclair. $12.95 paper, $35.00 cloth.

Still Alive: A Holocaust Girlhood Remembered by Ruth Kluger. $14.95 paper, $24.50 cloth.

Streets: A Memoir of the Lower East Side by Bella Spewack. $10.95 paper, $19.95 cloth.

Under the Rose: A Confession by Flavia Alaya. $15.95 paper, $29.95 cloth.

Vertigo by Louise DeSalvo. $15.95 paper.

Zulu Woman: The Life Story of Christina Sibiya by Rebecca Hourwich Reyer. $15.95 paper, $45.00 cloth.

To receive a free catalog of the Feminist Press's 200 titles, call or write the Feminist Press at the City University of New York, 365 Fifth Avenue, New York, NY 10016; phone: (212) 817-7920; fax: (212) 817-1593. Feminist Press books are available at bookstores or can be ordered directly at www.feministpress.org. Send check or money order (in U.S. dollars drawn on a U.S. bank) payable to the Feminist Press. Please add $4.00 shipping and handling for the first book and $1.00 for each additional book. VISA, MasterCard, and American Express are accepted for telephone and secure Internet orders. Prices subject to change.